CW01468419

Mr T

John Tiverton, senior physicist, returned home from work, opened his own front door—and encountered a wall of blankness. His wife and children did not know him, insisting he had died in a car crash six months before. A neighbour was equally uncompromising and tried to have him thrown out. Next day, when he sought help from his colleagues in the laboratory, they too insisted Tiverton was dead.

But if he was so anxious to prove his identity as Tiverton, why did he instinctively give the name Charles Thomas when booking into a small private hotel? Why did the freelance scientist Charles Thomas seem like an *alter ego*? What if he were really Thomas, hired to impersonate the brilliant Tiverton to cover up for something sinister? Was the real Mr T the one against whom there was a conspiracy to pronounce him dead, or the one who, having assumed another's identity, was unable to regain his own?

Mr T's efforts to establish himself as one or other led him into chilling danger and a thrilling across-London chase before he broke through to a convincing explanation. But was it convincing? Martin Russell here achieves a *tour de force* of characterization and a plot of uncanny brilliance.

by the same author

DUMMY RUN
HOUSE ARREST
THE SECOND TIME IS EASY
DEAD HEAT
PRIME TARGET
THE DARKER SIDE OF DEATH
CENSOR
A DOMESTIC AFFAIR
THE SEARCH FOR SARA
ALL PART OF THE SERVICE
RAINBLAST
BACKLASH
CATSPAW
DEATH FUSE
TOUCHDOWN
A DANGEROUS PLACE TO DWELL
DAYLIGHT ROBBERY
DIAL DEATH
DOUBLE DEAL
MURDER BY THE MILE
THE CLIENT
PHANTOM HOLIDAY
CRIME WAVE
DOUBLE HIT
CONCRETE EVIDENCE
ADVISORY SERVICE
DEADLINE
HUNT TO A KILL
DANGER MONEY
NO RETURN TICKET
NO THROUGH ROAD

MARTIN RUSSELL

Mr T

A Title in
THE DIAMOND JUBILEE COLLECTION

COLLINS, 8 GRAFTON STREET, LONDON W1

William Collins Sons & Co. Ltd
London · Glasgow · Sydney · Auckland
Toronto · Johannesburg

First published 1977
Reprinted in this Diamond Jubilee edition 1990
© Martin Russell 1977

ISBN 0 00 231545 9

Printed in Great Britain by
William Collins Sons & Co. Ltd, Glasgow

CHAPTER 1

As always, the atmosphere of the place had killed me off.

Someone at the Barton Street Library, someone in command, suffered from thin blood or static circulation and saw no reason for pandering at his own expense to the insane desire of others for breathable air. None of the windows opened. There were eight: lofty, mullioned affairs that ran the entire length of the rectangular reading-room on the fifth floor to cast debilitated light upon the central, refectory-style table and, as a superfluous by-product, to present a finely-chopped glimpse of the backs of buildings in Tottenham Court Road and the Post Office Tower beyond. Without them, and with air-conditioning, the room would have been much improved.

So, conceivably, would the female guardian of the filing system in her oaken nest by the exit. She had a baked, charred appearance, the unalterable result of too many years of over-cooking. I didn't want to look like that. I wanted to be able to study the *Theses* of Kummel without having to succumb to the opiate miasma that – as on former occasions – had overwhelmed me by the end of the second hour. Closing the book, I eased back my chair.

Despite all precautions, the legs grated noisily on the parquet flooring. The hooded orbs of the file clerk flickered my way, settling for an instant before refocusing upon their endless task at the file drawers. Nobody else stirred.

Maybe the heat had got them, too.

Rounding the bottom of the table with Kummel under an arm, I carried out a furtive examination of bowed heads. The only one I recognized was that of Walter Brent. He was in his usual place, assiduously adding to his already redoubtable intimacy with the laws of dynamics; he was writing – had been writing, the whisper went, for close on a decade – the definitive handbook on airframe tolerances; but each time completion was threatened, further discoveries were made which set him joyfully back a year. Walter was a happy man, obsessed with the notion that his work and mine in some way overlapped. It didn't, but I allowed him to imagine so; no harm was involved. I touched him as I passed.

'Still hard at it, I see.'

His face came up, moistly flushed from the heat and concentration. His eyes remained glazed: he was still among the pages. I gave him a compassionate grin. 'If I don't get out of here – ' my undertone seemed to reverberate from every corner – 'my hair's going to start singeing at the ends.' An inconsiderate quip, I thought belatedly, in view of Brent's total baldness.

He seemed to take it badly. There was no friendliness in his expression; unless he was uncommonly preoccupied with his subject, I had offended him. His eyeballs bulged in a somewhat repulsive manner. He said nothing. I placed a sustaining hand upon his right shoulder. 'Don't weaken – you've a textbook to write. But personally, I'm taking my work home.'

The arthritic, nicotine-stained forefinger of his left hand rested hunch-backed on a line of the page open before him, part of which was occupied by a diagram. Peering at it briefly, I gave him another grin, a knowing one. 'Sorry to interrupt.'

Heading for the door, I reflected that Walter was not getting any younger. If he was my senior by thirty years, as was rumoured, that made him sixty-seven; scarcely an age of senility, for all that. Perhaps it had been unfair to take him off-balance. There were times when I had been caught myself, deep in some cerebral commitment that had blinded me to external factors for the duration of its demands: on such occasions, recognition was slow to germinate. The next time I saw Walter, I decided, I should buy him a glass of his favourite brandy and apologize.

The file clerk glared at the Kummel as I lowered it to her burnished desk; then at me. I showed her portions of my teeth. 'I'd like to borrow this for a week, if I may.'

'What name?'

'Tiverton. John Tiverton.'

An odd thing, egotism. There was no particular reason why she should have known. Although I was not an infrequent visitor to the reading-room, the number of times I had actually taken out books could be reckoned on the fingers of a hand. But we all like to feel that we make a special impression. She looked at me for a second longer: her hand hovered with the library stamp above the flyleaf. At last it descended. Leaning upon it as though intent on bruising the paper, she raised it slightly to inspect the result.

'I shall have to charge a deposit. This is a specialist volume.'

I gave her a pound note. Slapping the hard cover back into place, she pushed the book across. I beamed into her arctic pupils. 'I'd have read it here, only your radiators were on the point of sending me to sleep.'

Perhaps she was the thin-blooded one. It was entirely possible that she possessed no blood of any kind. My remark went unacknowledged; she turned away to her filing cabinet without another glance, leaving me to depart like an admonished schoolboy from the head's study. I said, 'Thank you so much,' as ironically as possible. She paid no attention.

In the ground-floor entrance hall I ducked beneath the semi-elliptical Perspex above one of the pair of public telephones and dialled the Kaltmans number. An unfamiliar voice said she believed that Mr Simpson had left for the night.

'In case he hasn't,' I said, 'and you see him again, perhaps you wouldn't mind letting him know I've gone home direct from the library. Who is that?'

'It's the cleaner, sir.'

'Oh, I see. This is Mr Tiverton. If you should happen to get the chance, would you give him that message?'

'Right you are, sir. Who did you say?'

'Mr Tiverton.'

A pause. 'Right you are, sir,' she repeated like an incantation. 'Leave it with me.'

'Thank you.' I wrote her off. Hanging up, I left the stuffy building, pausing on the pavement outside for two reasons: to inhale the fume-laden but fresher air of early evening in a cool October, and to recall what it was that I had planned to buy on the way home. It had been, I felt, something rather vital.

CHAPTER 2

The door at the rear of the hall, on the right-hand side, was slightly ajar, releasing a spear of light and the sounds of cutlery scraping upon china, punctuated by Barbara' piping treble. 'Miss Townsend says we're to put our forks down the *other* way up.'

A mechanical note was discernible in Valerie's voice. 'Never mind what Miss Townsend says. You're at home now, you do as you're told.'

'Mummy. When c'n I go to school?'

'Michael, I keep telling you. First you have to be a little older, and after that . . .'

Fatigue notwithstanding, it was impossible not to smile. Entering the small lobby, I hung up my outer coat while stirring into a pile with one foot the books from Barbara's satchel that had leaked across the floor in the manner of surplus stock in a warehouse. I picked up a tiny mackintosh and hung it on its low-altitude peg. There was a smell of damp gaberdine. Shoes were everywhere. How had we reared a couple of centipedes? Back in the hall, I shoved the Kummel volume further to the back of the hatstand shelf and stood before the mirror, wearily dragging a comb through hair made sticky by atmospheric pollution or the Barton Street Library's boiler room. Barbara was now chattering about a friend called Katie.

A sustained clashing of china culminated in an abrupt broadening of the band of light as the living-room door was hooked inwards by a slippered foot. Valerie emerged, bearing a pile of plates. Without noticing me, she made for the kitchen on the other side of the hall: she was wearing her favourite sweater and slacks, and her dark hair was swept back and tied with a green band behind her head. She looked as tired as I felt. Pocketing the comb, I said softly, 'Hi there, beautiful.'

The plates hit the floor. One of them shattered, the pieces ricocheting from the skirting-board; another, intact, wheeled across the hall towards me. Falling short, it toppled to rest near the bottom stair. Valerie seemed hardly to notice what had happened. She stood staring towards me, her forehead contracted in a frown.

Stepping forward, I picked up the plate. 'Fair shot,' I observed. 'Up sights a little, perhaps. Then you'd have got me, fair and square.'

'I'm sorry.' Her voice sat on a higher note than usual. 'I didn't hear anyone come in. Was the door off the latch?'

'Door?' I turned to look back at the porch. 'If it was I didn't notice. Why?'

'Oh – you must be . . .' With a quick catch of the breath she advanced a few paces, studying me, the frown less obvious but still there, bridging her nose. 'You're rather late, aren't you? I've had no heating since mid-morning.'

'Oh no.' I groaned. 'Not that bloody gas boiler again.'

'That's why I called in to ask them to send somebody.' She spoke with a certain impatient severity. 'But I don't remember leaving the key.'

I said carefully, 'The key. Where?'

'At the showrooms, of course. When I went in about the boiler.'

I shook my head. 'Search me, love. I wasn't there.'

I took a pace towards her, holding out both arms. She seemed to recoil slightly. In a sharp way she said, 'Haven't you got any tools?'

'Why would I want tools? All that's needed is the touch of the master. If it doesn't respond to a spot of manipulation, there's nothing I can do with tools that would be of the slightest . . .' I paused, examining her more closely. Her attitude bothered me a little. 'Something up, darling? You seem jumpy.'

'I'm perfectly all right, thank you.' As she spoke, her inflection sharper than ever, she edged back towards the living-room door and tugged it fully into its frame with a soft thump, blotting out Michael's voice.

'Not allowed to see them tonight?' I put the question mildly, trying to estimate the magnitude of the domestic crisis that I had evidently landed in the middle of. Remaining where she was, Valerie made dusting movements with her fingertips on the hips of her trousers; it was a nervous habit that she had all but conquered. I said, 'I can tell you're on edge. Has the boiler exploded or something?'

'Not yet.' Her voice was frigid and flat, as though with suppressed anger. 'I don't want to rush you or anything, but since you're here, aren't you going to take a look?'

'Payment in advance,' I informed her. 'One kiss.'

She gave an impression of freezing where she stood.

'I don't want to have to call the police,' she said.

'Fat lot of good they'd be. Probably know less about boilers than I do.'

She gave a jerk of the head. 'The kitchen's that way.'

I looked at her for a moment. 'I hadn't forgotten.' She stiffened further. Something warned me off touching her at this stage; obviously it had been an exceedingly trying day. 'While I'm groping around,' I added, turning away, 'you can be pouring me a drink.'

On the way to the kitchen door I swung round. 'If you wouldn't mind,' I appended as a precaution.

From the same position in front of the door she was watching me, her posture suggestive of a scared chambermaid's. I tried to recall anything I had said at breakfast. While I was thinking, she spoke up in a rush. 'All right, I'll get you a drink.' She put a hand on the door handle but made no other move. With a shrug I continued into the kitchen.

'Rotten service in this establishment,' I called back.

Kneeling before the boiler, I pulled open the enamelled front and pondered the array of valves and taps before swivelling tap A to the left and switch B to the vertical. The latter movement was accompanied by a faint 'ting' which sounded remarkably like the lifting of a telephone receiver. I paused to listen. Valerie's voice became faintly audible: presumably she was speaking to the children. Undoubtedly she was in a strange mood. I hoped a quiet drink together would help to sort things out. In the meantime I had no matches. Getting to my feet, I searched the wall-cupboard where they were kept. A noise from the door made me turn.

'What is it you're looking for?' Valerie enquired. The flat quality of her voice was even more pronounced.

'Something to light the pilot with.'

Silently she crossed to the table, extracted a box from the drawer and lobbed them at me. They bounced off my left palm to the floor.

'Thanks terribly.' I spoke with ironic effusion, stooping to retrieve them while she watched stonily. Returning to my knees, I made a few thrusts with a lighted match, igniting the pilot jet at the fifth attempt. I flipped the controls. The boiler got under way with a whump.

I stood. 'That'll cost you a dry martini. Plus the peck on the cheek I applied for and never got.'

Valerie had returned to the doorway to stand regarding the now humming boiler with a neutral expression. At my words she took a couple of hasty steps backwards into the hall.

'I think,' she said tightly, 'you'd better be leaving now.' I followed her slowly out of the kitchen.

'If this is some joke you've cooked up with the kids,' I began, 'I wish you'd let them come out and enjoy it. Speaking for myself, I've had a long and exhausting – '

The slam of the porch door interrupted me. A heavily-built man of about my own age tramped into the hall, pausing at the street end to survey the two of us. Gulping down the rest of my original sentence, I changed course. 'Hullo,' I said, not too amicably. 'What brings you here, the sound of raised voices?'

Approaching us at a deliberate stride, he planted himself at Valerie's elbow, inspecting me with his rather close-set eyes under a trendy fringe. His jutting chin was raised appraisingly. From wide shoulders his arms hung loosely at his sides. It occurred to me that I had never realized before how bellicose our nearest neighbour was capable of looking. Without removing his gaze he said, 'What's he been up to?'

'Nothing really, Tom.' Valerie was perceptibly short of breath. 'I just . . . wanted you around.'

'Is he making a nuisance of himself?'

'Not to any extent, but . . . Would you mind asking him to leave?'

He folded his arms across his chest. 'We both heard the lady.'

'Don't you think,' I asked Valerie, 'this has progressed beyond a joke?'

'Mister, it's been made fairly clear. Your presence here isn't wanted by Mrs Tiverton. So would you care to oblige?'

I turned on him. 'Just what do you think you're on, Elkins? Get out of my house.'

He released a snigger in Valerie's direction. '"Get out of my house",' he mimicked. 'Said that pretty well, didn't he? You've got a bloody nerve,' he added, staring at me with a cold contempt.

I addressed myself to her. 'Darling, I've stood all I can. It's not funny any more, if it ever was. I've had a hard day: I'm shattered. Tell Tom to get back to his supper and for Christ's sake let me have a bath.'

Glances travelled between them. Elkins moved closer to me.

'There's the door.' He gestured.

'You don't want us to call the police?' Valerie spoke in a kind of hushed gasp.

Elkins stood between me and the staircase. I brushed him aside, feeling the solidity of his frame. 'I've had about a skinful of this nonsense. I'll be upstairs for a while. If you want to stop for a drink, Elkins, help yourself, and pour a long one for me. Probably I'll feel livelier by the time I come down.'

I reached the third stair before I was wrenched back.

'Mister, you couldn't have heard. That's the way to the door. See? Over there.'

'Get your hands off me.'

'Okay. Soon as you're the far side of that street door.'

'Val – tell him to lay off. Want me to belt him one?'

She was moving away towards the living-room, a hand to her mouth. I tried to follow. 'Val, for Pete's sake! How far does this have to – '

The back of Elkins's fleshy hand hit me across the mouth. I reeled against the nearest wall, only to be held by his grasp and hauled upright again. His eyes were hard and cold.

'That's it, then,' he said between his teeth. 'You asked for it.'

'Don't hurt him, Tom.'

'Don't worry, love. It's the only thing they understand.'

One of my arms was free. Bringing it round hard, I buried my fist in his stomach. With an explosive grunt he jabbed a handful of rigid fingers upwards into my throat, knocking the wind out of me so that all I could do was stand there and heave for breath while he held on. 'Lost your chance, mister,' he said into my right ear. 'You don't leave now.'

CHAPTER 3

From where I sat I could see his broad neck, with its surplus pleats, reflected by the mirror in the back of the archaic oaken dresser which Valerie had inherited from a great-aunt who died at Worthing. Without intending to keep it, we had found ourselves stuck with it; twice it had moved house with us, tagging along like an unwanted but mutely persistent elder relative. I found myself studying it in detail for the first time. Normally this front room of the house was barely used unless we had guests, which was seldom. It seemed alien to me. The house was silent. If the children were still in the adjoining living-room, Valerie was keeping them steadfastly in order. Elkins was chewing at something, gazing through the window at the street lighting.

I moved in the chair. The chewing stopped.

'Want something?'

'Yes,' I said shakily. 'An explanation.'

'Ah, too right. You'll be needing one.'

'You know what I mean.'

With a slight smile he started masticating again; a rhythmic circular motion of the jaws. I turned my head so that I didn't have to watch.

'Elkins,' I said presently. 'Tell me something. Have you gone completely mad?'

The chewing suspended itself again. 'Do me a favour?'

he requested. 'Cut out the injured innocence. Makes me sick.'

From its perch at one end of the dresser, the eight-day chiming clock that had been a wedding gift from Valerie's parents commenced a laborious clearing of its throat, preparatory to announcing the hour by means of seven tinny gongs. Comparing his watch, Elkins made an adjustment to the winder and held it to his ear.

'Tell Valerie,' I said, 'I want to see her.'

He wound the watch a few times, giving it all his attention.

I raised my voice to a shout. 'Valerie!'

Taking four rapid steps across the room, he struck my face with the flat of his hand. 'I'm not warning you again,' he said conversationally. 'One more peep out of you and I'll be using my knuckles. Now watch it.'

Turning his back on me, he strolled back to the dresser.

I rested my face on my hands. Between the fingers I could see that the carpet had been freshly Hoovered: the pile was erect, wearing a faint gloss. Carpets always looked like that when Valerie had been over them with the Hoover.

Elkins wore slippers. Light brown, with elastic sides. A zipped woollen waistcoat in a similar colour covered a yellow shirt. He had taken up his former position, spine to the mirror, leaning backwards with his weight on both elbows; his hands were crossed against his stomach, the thick fingers entwined. I thought, vaguely, that I should be throwing myself at him, manhandling him from the premises. If Valerie had asked me to, I wouldn't have hesitated.

The clock's monotonous ticking faltered and recovered. The hands stood at three minutes past seven. I lifted my head as another sound intruded: a brief expiring swish from the street, followed by a slam. Elkins became alert. Pushing himself upright, he adopted a listening pose. There was a double ring at the street door. The instant opening of the living-room door was followed by rapid footsteps along the hall, and then a muddle of voices from which Valerie's – quivering slightly to betray tension – eventually emerged more distinctly. 'He's in here.'

The door opened with a rattle, revealing her strained face. She threw me the briefest flicker of a glance before turning back to usher through a uniformed police-sergeant, a slim man of middle age with an intelligent air about him. For a second or two he stood looking my way, then addressed himself to Elkins. 'No further trouble, sir?'

'None to speak of.'

They all studied me. At last the sergeant turned to Valerie. 'Announced himself as . . .?'

'The gas man. At least that's who I took him to be. I came out of the living-room and there he was, standing in the hall.'

'Mm.' The sergeant circled, inspecting me covertly from different angles. 'Never seen him before?'

'Never. He's a total stranger to me.'

I had planned to say nothing for a while, to let them do the talking while I established an impression of saneness and sobriety that might stand me in good stead later. But this was too much. I came to my feet, feeling my head swim as though I were standing at the tail of an airliner in a storm. 'Look here, this is utterly – '

'Did he molest you?' asked the sergeant.

'In a way. It's a bit hard to describe. His behaviour was most odd.'

'I see.' The sergeant's percipient eyes were directed

fully at me. 'Well: can't have that, can we?'

Elkins said, 'I think we should bring a charge.'

Valerie looked upset. 'It hardly seems serious enough to – '

'If we overlooked this,' he explained, 'he might try it on again. And it could be worse next time. Isn't that right, Sergeant?'

'It's a possibility,' he agreed solemnly.

Valerie chewed her lower lip. She kept looking at me as though she were trying to discover some mitigating factor in a course of conduct that was fundamentally beyond her; then glancing away before I had time to capitalize on the contact. I sensed a lack of sympathy between the sergeant and Elkins. Holding on to the windowsill for support, I said, 'Do you mind if I say a thing or two on my own behalf?'

'Go ahead, old man,' said the sergeant invitingly.

My limbs had begun to shake out of control. 'In the first place,' I told him through chattering teeth, 'I want the children brought in here . . .'

Valerie began a vigorous shaking of the head. Elkins said, 'They're best kept out of the – '

'Why d'you ask that?' queried the sergeant.

'Why? Because I happen to be their father, that's why. I trust I'm not being unreasonable.'

'They're your children?'

'That's another way of putting it.'

'Mrs Tiverton?' He turned to her. 'Any special objection?'

'What, to their being brought in? Well, I have, yes. I don't see why they should become involved. My little girl's been frightened already by the noise. They both ought to be in bed. There's absolutely no reason why this man – '

'I'm her husband,' I told the sergeant. 'This woman speaking to you is my wife. She's my wife, I tell you.'

'He's a nutcase,' said Elkins.

'This man,' I said, jabbing a thumb at him, 'has lived in the house next door for several months. Tom Elkins: that's his name. He works at a travel bureau in Hampstead. Each morning at around eight-thirty he takes off in a Toyota. Back in July he paid a working visit to Bulgaria and came home via Munich. His wife Gillian hasn't got a job, but she – '

'Any of this,' Elkins said scornfully, 'he could have dug up by making a few inquiries.'

I pointed to Valerie. 'She's thirty-two next April. We married at Croydon in May, 'sixty-eight. Before moving here we lived at Purley. Our daughter Barbara is seven and a half years old; Michael will be four next month. I call my wife Val except when we argue: then I call her Scamp. Her mother died three years ago. Her father – '

The sergeant elevated a quenching hand. 'I don't think we need go into all that.'

'But don't you see? It's essential if I'm to – '

'Whether or not you're this lady's husband should be easy enough to confirm. You say you are; she says you're not. Mr Elkins here says you're not. Now the first thing we have to – '

I planted myself in front of him. 'Just eleven hours ago I left this house to go to work. I had breakfast in the living-room on the other side of that wall they're standing against. Kippers. If you look in the scrap bin you'll probably find the bones. Kippers, toast and coffee. Right, Val? Then I said goodbye to the kids. Mike threw a tantrum as I left, but it was soon over and he waved goodbye from the porch.' I stared at Valerie. 'Have I left anything out?'

Her face was averted. After a pause the sergeant said politely, 'Have you anything that will identify you?'

Searching my pockets, I found my wallet. He turned it out on the dresser.

'Jottings book. Can't make out what's written here – nothing legible. A fiver and three pound notes. This all you carry?'

'Driving licence. Not there?'

Upending the wallet, he shook it. Nothing more dropped out. Carefully replacing the notes, he returned it to me.

I said, 'There might be something in my overcoat pockets.'

'Where's that?'

'Outside in the lobby. A light grey woollen job with a quilted lining. You can't miss it.'

'Hold on.' He left the room.

While we waited I sat on the windowsill, breathing steadily in an attempt to give myself some backbone and put an end to the dizziness. I didn't look at the others and they disregarded me. Valerie busied herself with winding the clock. An unnecessary task, since I had wound it myself two nights previously. Elkins, whistling under his breath, became engrossed in an inspection of his nails. After some delay the sergeant returned with the coat, its pocket linings protruding on both sides.

I said, 'Did you find anything?'

With a shake of the head he indicated the linings. 'Seems you're in the habit of travelling light.'

Valerie said, 'Do we have to go solemnly through all this? It's absurd. I've told you – I've never seen this man before.'

The sergeant pivoted slowly. 'He does seem to know quite a bit about you, Mrs Tiverton.'

She shook her head in a helpless fashion. Her gaze
returned to me.

I lifted my shoulders. 'What am I supposed to say?
"I'm her husband" seems to cut no ice. What else is there?'

'I'll tell you what else.' Elkins's voice was harsh with
contempt. 'The whole thing is in bloody poor taste.'

The sergeant's head took on a tilt.

'I mean,' said Elkins, 'for someone in Mrs Tiverton's
position . . .'

Valerie took him up in a level voice. 'What Mr Elkins
is referring to, Sergeant, is that I'm a widow. My husband
died six months ago.'

CHAPTER 4

'. . . does throw a different light on things . . .'

'Watch him, he's going to fall.'

'He's faking.'

'. . . understand his motives. Not as though he . . .'

'I reckon he's putting it on.'

'. . . advisable to bring him round. We don't want to
have to . . .'

'Beyond comprehension.'

The final two words boomed around the room. From
the way they were all looking at me, I judged that I had
uttered them. They had a good, crisp, authoritative sound,
so I said them again. This time their echo was duller.
I lost interest in the phrase: it seemed to be leading no-
where. The sergeant was talking. 'Feel up to getting on
your feet?'

'I want this looked into,' I said earnestly as he helped
me up. 'Looked right into.'

'Don't you worry, sir.'

I hunted with my eyes. 'Where is she now?'

'Mrs Tiverton's gone back to the living-room. Don't want her bothered again, do we?'

'Valerie! Come here a moment!'

'Knock it off, old man.'

'I insist on seeing her. I demand to be – '

'Come on now. I don't want to have to behave like a policeman.'

'Val! It's a joke, isn't it? A lousy rotten legpull. Tell him it's over. Can't you see what it's done to me? You've overshot the – '

'Unless you button your lip, you know, I'll have to do it for you.'

'Be as lenient as you can, Sergeant.' She stood in the living-room doorway, distress in her attitude, as we passed through the hall. 'I don't believe he quite realizes . . . Look, I've brought this.'

Taking the print from her, he squinted at it for a few seconds before showing it to me. Set in a frame of wood and glass with a hinged support at the back, it showed in half-profile a youngish, lean-faced man with light, thinning hair, a sharp nose and a slightly receding chin. He had worn a dark sweater and an open-necked shirt when the photograph was taken. 'Val, with all my love, John.' The words were written in ink in a slanting hand at the base.

After a moment the sergeant said gently, 'It's not – is it?'

I stabbed two fingers at the print. 'That's not me.'

'No,' he concurred.

'I mean . . . it's not *me*. Don't you understand? Someone has . . . That's the wrong photograph.'

'A different one,' he corrected.

I kept my gaze on the print as though if I stared long enough the facial features would obligingly blur and re-form. Presently the sergeant took it out of my fingers and handed it back to Valerie. I stood looking ahead. Beyond the half-open door of the kitchen, the figure of Elkins was both visible and audible: he seemed to be preparing coffee.

'There's just one thing . . .' The sergeant was peering at Valerie. 'You said you found this gentleman in the hall . . . how did he get there? I mean, how did he get into the house?'

'I can only think,' she said slowly, 'I left the lock of the door on the catch when I came in with the children. Then it just needs a push.'

'There's no question of his having a key?'

'As far as I know, there are only two in existence. One's in my purse and the other on the kitchen shelf.'

'Fetch them both here, would you?'

While we waited for her the sergeant sent some appreciative glances around the hall and up the stairway. It was an attractive entrance to the house; I had always admired it myself. Catching my eye, he gave a small self-conscious smile. 'House lay-outs interest me,' he remarked. 'I live in a flat myself.'

'Here you are,' said Valerie, returning.

He lined both keys up on a palm. Taking them to the street door, he tested each one successfully. He brought them back. 'Look after them,' he told Valerie, returning them to her. 'Awkward if they strayed.'

'One of those,' I said, 'is mine.'

He regarded me kindly. 'That we can sort out in due course. For the time being Mrs Tiverton had better hold on to the pair.'

'You realize you're locking me out of my own house?'

'Now come along.'

'Where to?'

'Sergeant . . .' She spoke breathlessly. 'I'd sooner this was taken no further.'

'Up to you, madam. You made the complaint.'

'Yes, well – I was a bit shaken. But I don't think he meant any harm. He's confused, isn't he? Let him go.'

'He might annoy you again.'

'I shouldn't think so. I'm willing to chance it.'

The sergeant looked inscrutable. 'Just the same,' he announced at last, 'I'll see him well off the premises. Will Mr Elkins be around for a while longer?'

'I'm sure he'll stay if I ask him.'

'I'll be here,' Elkins called from the kitchen.

'Right you are, old man.' The sergeant handed me my overcoat. 'Shall we get going without any fuss?'

The constable was tall and young; barely into his twenties by the look of him. He stood next to me alongside the patrol car, his demeanour insecure. The sergeant had instructed him to keep an eye on me and then had walked off, covering twenty yards of footway before turning in through the gate of the next house along the street in the opposite direction to that of the Elkins. His footwear echoed from a concrete path.

The evening air was sharp. I thrust myself into the overcoat, helped ineffectually by the constable with an air of bending the rules. A motor-cyclist chuntered by, snorting the engine in spasms and getting a hard look from the law. As he puttered out of earshot the sergeant came walking back: his junior relaxed.

'Well now.' The sergeant confronted me, his face a shade of putty under the lamps. 'Let's have your name.'

'Tiverton. John Tiverton.'

He sighed. 'Gentleman of that name, who lived here, died half a year ago. I've just confirmed that with a neighbour.'

'I'm John Tiverton.'

'He was cremated at Malling Road.'

'I'm John Tiverton and I live at that house.'

'Mrs Tiverton's been a widow for six months. What was your purpose in gaining admittance?'

'You mean why did I go inside? I came home. I'd been to work.'

'Where?'

'Kaltmans Industrial. Kilburn.'

'What as?'

'Research metallurgist. Did she tell you the same?'

'Who?'

'Miss Cardelaine. The neighbour you've just spoken to.'

'So you know her name?'

'I've been calling her by it for two years.'

He meditated. 'Who's your boss?'

'A man called Simpson. Melville Simpson.'

'Know his home address or number?'

'I could look it up.'

Leaning past me, he tugged open the rear door of the patrol car. 'Get in.'

He sat beside me while the constable drove. During the ten-minute journey we exchanged no further remarks: the sergeant seemed to be as intent upon traffic conditions as the man at the wheel, uttering an occasional growl at the antics of other motorists. On arrival they escorted me up some steps, through a pair of swing doors into a reception office and from there to a smaller room at the rear, reached by means of a heavy door veneered with plastic walnut that on release was forced back into the frame by a hydraulic device that hissed with the exertion.

They left me there while they went for directories.

Along two walls were ranged dark green metal file cabinets. Against a third stood an oblong table bearing a telephone. There were three chairs, precariously-based structures of tubular steel that oscillated under pressure. I sat on one.

From the outer office came the subdued note of the duty sergeant's deep voice, phlegmatically helpful: it sounded like a case of assault. A woman was explaining something. I envied her the ability. The way I felt, nothing would ever be explicable again. Her lifeless monotone began to rasp on my nerves; covering both ears, I sat forward with elbows on the table and stared at the grain of the wood.

'Managed to find the right book,' said the sergeant's mellower baritone above my head. I looked up. 'They get shoved out of sight,' he complained, thumbing the leaves. 'Never the same place twice running. Simpson, you said? Eden Vale . . . Here we are. Simpson, Melville, High View. That the chappie?' I nodded. He lifted the phone.

From where I sat I could hear the ringing tone. It continued unanswered for half a minute: he glanced down at me, raising his eyebrows. I said, 'He's out quite often. If there's no reply, the thing to do – '

'Hullo?' he interrupted. 'I wonder if I might speak to Mr Simpson. Not there? When will he be in, d'you know? Not till tomorrow *evening*? Is it possible by any chance to contact him before then?'

He listened. Presently he said, 'Would you mind holding the line?' Masking the mouthpiece, he glanced back at me. 'Your Mr Simpson's on a business trip – not available till about this time tomorrow. It's his housekeeper. Want a word with her?'

I took over the receiver. 'Good evening. We haven't
met, but you may possibly have heard my name from Mr
Simpson. I'm John Tiverton, a colleague of his at Kaltmans.'

She sounded anxious to please, but dubious. 'I'm not
too well up on Mr Simpson's friends, sir, I must admit.
Is there a message I can pass on?'

'I was hoping to speak to him. It's most urgent. Can't
he be contacted?'

'I wouldn't know where he is, sir.' She sounded honest.
'He's not at his office, that I do know, because I've tried
there myself a couple of times. He did tell me he'd be away
for the night. All I can suggest – '

'Right.' I spoke with a brusqueness born of fatigue and
frustration and stress. 'If he should happen to come in,
would you ask him . . .' I paused. 'No, that's not much
good. I might try again later.'

'Yes, sir, right you are then.' After a moment's hesitation
she put down the phone. I did the same.

'No go?' asked the sergeant neutrally.

'Seems things are against me.' Numbness was crawling
over my brain; I fought it off. 'There's someone else we
could try.'

He passed me the directory. 'Find the number for
yourself,' he said without expression.

After a few moments' search I handed the book back,
indicating with a finger. 'Selby . . . Frank Selby. He's a
senior colleague of mine. I don't think he goes out a lot
in the evenings.'

Without comment he relayed the number to the switchboard.

There was a minimal pause before the receiver reso-
nated. He said smoothly, 'Mr Selby? Sorry to trouble you,
sir. This is Waller Grove Police Station, Sergeant Barker

speaking. No, no, nothing alarming. But you might be able to help us on a small matter. I understand you're with Kaltmans Industrial. Yes. Can you tell me, sir, have you a colleage there by the name of Tiverton?

'I see. Six months ago.

'Has he been replaced? I see.

'Yes, of course. Um . . . can you describe roughly what Mr Tiverton looked like?

'Uh-huh. And his replacement?

'Thank you, sir, that's all I wanted to know. Nothing whatever to do with the firm. Purely a question of identity. We've a gentleman here, claims to be Tiverton. No resemblance, no. Very sorry to have disturbed you. You've been extremely – '

Reaching up, I snatched the receiver from him. He said 'Hey', but made no move to reclaim it; merely looked on while I spoke. 'Frank,' I said urgently, 'is that you?'

'Who's that?'

'It's John. John Tiverton, you nitwit. Don't you recognize my voice?'

'What's all this supposed to be – '

'Listen a moment. It's vital we sort this out. When I got home an hour or two ago – '

'Look,' he said on a high, querulous note, 'I've no idea who you are and I'm not interested. For what it's worth, and whatever it has to do with you, all I can say is that John Tiverton used to work at Kaltmans until he was killed a few months back – '

'*Killed?*'

'Yes, in a road crash. There was – '

'God, man, I was with you this morning. What's up with everybody?'

'This morning?' His voice was utterly blank. 'I was by myself the whole time.'

'You must remember.' Frantically I searched my memory. 'We were talking about – well, the usual problem, and I mentioned I was planning to beetle off to the library this afternoon and try Kummel. Which is what I did. I spent three hours there and finally took the book out because it was hard to concentrate and too stuffy. Then when I arrived home – '

'You're just wasting my time.' He said it, I thought, cagily. 'Put me back to the sergeant, will you?'

'Frank, for Christ's sake. I need your help. Something seems to have happened to Val – she says she doesn't know me, refuses to have me in the house . . .'

The receiver clicked. Selby had hung up.

The right hand of Sergeant Barker swooped gently and took the instrument back. He replaced it meticulously on its rest.

'Now suppose we stop all this nonsense. Where d'you live?'

'We've just come from there.'

He shook a sad head. 'You'd better clear off. Before I think up something to do with you. Get a night's sleep. Think matters over.'

'I want to make another call.'

'What d'you think this is, a charity post office?'

'Long-distance: to Newcastle.' I slapped a pound note on the table. 'That ought to cover it.'

'I need my head examined,' he said, making no move.

The switchboard girl told me to wait. Presently she said, 'Go ahead, you're through.'

'Hullo?' My voice cracked with tension. I had to clear my throat. 'Mrs Tiverton?'

'Who's that speaking?' The voice came thin and high along the wires.

'John, Mother. So sorry to worry you. It's nothing

really, only I – '

'John who?'

I gripped hard at the receiver. Slowly and distinctly I said, 'That is Mrs Tiverton?'

'Yes.'

'Well . . . it's me, John.'

Sergeant Barker rested part of his weight against a metal cabinet, regarding me dispassionately. There was no sound from Newcastle. I ploughed on against the silence. 'I'm phoning because I seem to have hit a spot of bother. Val's behaving strangely. She doesn't appear to know me, and when I – '

'I think you must have the wrong number.'

Her voice was dead, like a chanting priest's. Suddenly it became important to me to conceal what was happening from the sergeant. He mustn't know. I said briskly, 'Where's Dad? Fetch Dad to the phone, will you?'

'Please ring off and stop bothering us.'

'Mother, it's me. *John.*'

After a long pause she spoke again on a breath of a sob. 'My son has been dead for six months. I don't know who you are, but please get off the line.'

The receiver at the other end clattered against something. A moment later it was gently replaced.

Returning to the table, Sergeant Barker pulled open a small drawer, extracted a tube of peppermints and held them out. Retracting his hand after an interval, he tore away part of the wrapping and took one himself. His mouth began forming odd shapes.

'Hear what I said just now? A night's sleep. You'll be surprised, the difference it makes.'

'I want to see the Commissioner.'

'The which?'

'The top man. Whoever's in charge. I want an interview with him.'

He leaned over the table, sucking at me. 'Far as you're concerned, old man, I'm the little tin god you have to worship. Even the Prime Minister can't make you something you're not.'

I stared past him at the wall, talking dreamily. 'She calls me Jimmy sometimes: God knows why. It's not my name. There's six thousand nine hundred-odd owing on the house. She's got a birthmark on the inside of her left thigh. Weighs eight-three, stands five-five. Barbara's middle name is Mary. Mike's is Paul. They both hate cheese.'

The sergeant's mouth had come to a halt about the peppermint.

'Val and I met through my work. She was in a Government department. Character assessment and screening . . . the sort of thing she was good at. After we were married they asked her to carry on. Then she left to have Barby. She likes being a housewife and a mother. At least I think she does. Maybe she hankers after her old job. Maybe – '

'Listen. Are you going to get out of here?'

'She hasn't seemed restless . . .'

'Or force me to take some action? I can, you know. Insulting behaviour. Disturbance likely to cause a breach. Anything. If you go back to that house. I'm warning you.'

'It's my house. Our house.'

He straightened officially. 'You've been cautioned. Don't say you've not. Now buzz off.'

CHAPTER 5

The constable tailed me clumsily at a distance until I reached the bus shelter. Then he killed time, unconvincingly trying a few shop door handles, until a bus grunted along and I stepped aboard. Its route was far removed from my own territory. Looking back from the tail-deck, I saw him turn and stride off, back towards the station, there to report on the triumphant completion of his mission.

Paying for a tenpenny ticket, I stayed on the lower deck for five stops. At a brightly-lit thoroughfare I got off.

Spears of fine rain pierced the glow of the street lamps. The only sign of life came from a discotheque on the opposite side of the road, spilling its noisy glitter over the wet tarmac. Crossing, I stood outside for a few minutes, listening to the uproar coming from inside. A youth and a girl emerged, wearing identical hairstyles and matching denim suits with buttons everywhere; the girl's face was matt-white and her lashes probed ahead like curved antennae. As they set off along the pavement his right hand fondled her rump while she rotated a hip against his. I followed them until I came to a bus stop, the counterpart of the one at which I had alighted. I stood there and waited. The couple moved on, out of sight.

A number of cars splashed past at more or less regular intervals, as hypnotic as a metronome. Finally a bus groaned out of the drizzle and picked me up.

By the time I got off, the rain had almost stopped.

I walked carefully but quickly along the slippery footway, hearing the slap-slap of my shoes echoing from the
house-fronts. A few windows betrayed light behind drawn
curtains, but it was not until I came level with our own
property that I saw radiance splashing the garden path.
It came from the glazed door inside the porch. There was
no sign of movement.

Turning in through the gate, I kept to the grass,
skirting bushes, staying in shadow as far as possible until
I was beyond the porch and continuing along the side
of the house. At the halfway point I tripped over something that scraped metallically over the flagstones. It
was Barbara's bicycle. Picking it up, I propped it back
against the wall before edging the remaining three yards
to the outer door of the kitchen and testing the lever handle.
The door was bolted from the inside.

At the rim of the flagstones nearby stood the toolshed.
The ladder was on its rack on the side facing the house.
Lifting it off, I caught the brickwork a solid blow with
one end; I paused, holding my breath, but nothing
stirred. After a thirty-second delay I carried the ladder
round to the rear patio and leaned it half-length against
the top of the wooden loggia.

I went up at a rung a minute. My soles seemed to
scrape like carpenter's files; at one point the base of the
ladder swivelled abruptly before finding a new grip,
sending me against an upright with my heart in my
mouth. At the top I rested before tackling the cross-
beam linking the upright with the wall. It was sturdy
six-inch timber, but in the near-darkness I had no sense
of balance and had to do it on hands and knees, clinging
with all my strength until I was within range of the
bedroom window and could reach out and steady myself.
I waited while my nerve came back. Then I stretched

upwards, found a gap in the fanlight and inserted three fingers.

With the metal frame cutting into my flesh, I pulled myself to a standing position from which I could work the rest of my arm inside and reach the fastener of the main window. With a slight grating sound it came free. Pulling the window wide, I raised a leg and swung it across the sill, heaving the remainder of my body after it. For a moment I sat straddled, peering into the room.

I lowered myself to the floor.

Barbara hadn't stirred. Even when I crossed the carpet to the switch and illuminated the room she remained motionless under the bedclothes, only her flaxen hair and a curve of cheek visible on the pillow. I stood looking at the little mound for a moment: then I sat on the edge of the mattress, bouncing it. Placing a hand on the sheet around her shoulder, I spoke her name softly, twice.

She gave a tiny sigh. I shook her gently.

Sliding a hand between her hair and the pillow, I lifted her face. Her eyes twitched in the glare from the bulb. I raised her to a sitting position.

'Barby,' I said in her ear. 'Barby, are you awake?'

Her eyes came fully open. She blinked several times.

She said, 'Hallo, Daddy.'

The door plunged back, hitting the bed. Elkins said, 'You again. What the hell do you think you're up to?'

Apparently about to leap at me, he paused irresolute, looking at the child. 'Put her down. Get away from her.'

I stared back at him with a cold fury. 'When I choose. Who do you think you are, giving orders?'

'You heard me. Leave go of her.'

Valerie called from the stairs. 'What is it, Tom?'

'It's him again. The nutcase. He's here in Barbara's bedroom.'

'What!'

'Get on to the police – fast.'

Her hasty steps descended to the hall. I glanced down at Barbara, who was studying me in drowsy puzzlement; I said 'Sorry, love,' gave her a quick kiss and laid her back, then rose and moved towards Elkins in the doorway. 'I want a word with Valerie. Get out of my way.'

His eyelids flickered: he was thinking. Slowly he moved aside, giving me room to pass by him to the landing. As I took a step towards the top stair his hand grabbed me by a sleeve and I was yanked round. I had thought I was prepared, but he moved quickly: seeing his fist arriving, I made a belated attempt to dodge and took a glancing blow to the side of the head which spun me against the banister. Since he was still holding me by the other hand he came along too, pinning me to the woodwork.

Downstairs, the telephone bell gave out half a ring. Elkins had his thumbs on my throat; his eyes glared into mine. I tried to bring up a knee, but his weight was distributed over me so that I was pinned in all quarters. The thumbs altered position, searching with a vicious deliberation for my larynx. His face swung away as he raised his voice: 'Tell them to send a squad car with a couple of men and not to waste any – '

My right leg came free. Hooking it behind him, I thrust forward, sending both of us staggering clear of the banister to the top of the staircase. The back of his skull came into contact with the wall, bringing a grunt from him and a momentary relaxation of the thumb-pressure which I exploited by jerking back my head and simultaneously kicking out with my free foot, feeling the impact against his shin-bone. His cry of pain filled me with

fierce delight. I was out of his bear-hug, able to aim blows
at his face. Down in the hall, Valerie was talking to
someone in a high urgent voice.

Elkins began to hit back. For a moment or two we
stood slugging it out like a pair of novice welterweights,
most of the blows coming to nothing on arms or shoulders.
Inside the bedroom Barbara was crying, calling for her
mother. The sound of her gave me an instant's extra
strength, and a right-handed jab got through to his jutting
chin. He had his back to the staircase at the time; my
punch was solid enough to rob him of balance, sending
him backwards with flailing arms that found nothing to
clutch. The staircase was a straight flight to the ground
floor. He went down head-first on his spine, bumping
from stair to stair, coming to rest in an untidy position
on the hall carpet and staying there, motionless, his head
at an angle to the rest of him.

Valerie and I arrived together. She stood gazing down
at him, then up at me, horror dawning in her eyes.
'What have you done to him?' she asked.

I could find nothing to say. She began to retreat
towards the lobby, both arms clasping her waist as though
she was in pain. Watching her, I tried to manufacture
words; I had lost the knack. All I was good for was
movement, a crablike progress that developed into a
stride as I went past her to the street door, brushing her
out of the way, sending her reeling. The drizzle had
renewed itself: it came spikily into my face as I left the
house.

CHAPTER 6

In a street near the Victoria Coach Station I rang at a door beneath a square wall-lamp which had 'Hotel' painted on three sides, and was reached by means of steps between iron railings. Plants straggled out of a box of earth arranged on legs to the right of the top step. There was a brief delay before the door was eased back by a slim woman in slacks who gave me a friendly smile. 'Are you after a room?'

'Just for tonight,' I said.

She puckered her lips. 'All I could offer . . . Step inside a moment, will you?'

I followed her into the narrow passage. From where we stood, it led through to a doorway on a slightly lower level, beyond which was a glimpse of a comfortable-looking room with television sounds coming from it.

'There's just an attic room on the top floor,' she said, inspecting me frankly. 'Strictly speaking it hasn't been cleared for fire risk, but if you don't mind taking the chance . . .'

'I've no objection.'

'So long as it's somewhere to sleep?' The smile came again. 'I think you'll find it quite adequate. Just arrived in London?'

'Down from the Midlands. Had a car accident on the way,' I explained. 'Lost all my luggage.'

Her face lengthened expressively, the way Valerie's could. 'Oh my goodness. Was anyone hurt?'

'No, I was lucky. Just piled into a ditch.'

'I expect now you're getting the reaction?'

'I expect I am.'

She turned decisively. 'I'll see if I can find you some old pyjamas of my husband's. Wait here a minute.'

She marched away through the rear doorway and disappeared. The passage in which I stood was decorated, walls and ceiling, with heavily embossed paper painted a glossy cream; a long, slender table against one wall was strewn with uncollected mail and Guides to London. There was a loitering scent of roast potatoes. From the street outside came the note of an engine, the swish of tyres against kerbstones; then silence. My muscles tautened. Presently a car door slammed. I was starting to edge for the street entrance when the woman returned, looking businesslike.

'I've put them to warm for a few minutes in front of the fire. Meanwhile I'll show you the room, Mr . . .?'

'Thomas. Charles Thomas.'

'I'm Mrs Carpenter. Let me give you one of our cards.' She handed me one from the table. 'We're a bit over-active at present – the usual autumn rush – but as a rule we can take anyone at short notice. Handy to know. Mind these stairs, you might find them rather steep. Sorry it's such a drag up. Dare say you're feeling stiff. Have you seen a doctor?'

'Doctor?'

'Since you had the accident.' Her voice held an odd note: it occurred to me that my own had been unwarrantably curt. I gave her a smile as she negotiated a turning above me.

'Oh no. It didn't seem necessary. I was only shaken.'

'But you should have been X-rayed.' In deference to other residents she had lowered her voice.

I said, 'I might think about it tomorrow.'

'If you'd care for a bath, there's one there . . .' She pointed as we passed. 'And another on the floor below your room.'

A steeper flight of stairs from the third floor took us to a cupboard-like door which opened into a small bedroom with sloped ceilings. She switched on a light. 'Hilary should have left the window open,' she observed, sniffing. 'Stuffy in here.' She went across to release the catch. 'Will this suit you?'

The room was neatly papered and carpeted. The bed looked level. A washbasin stood in an alcove. 'Fine,' I said. 'All I want.'

'I'm afraid I shall have to ask for payment in advance.'

'Yes, of course.'

'It's four pounds for the night. That includes breakfast.' She accepted my five-pound note. 'I'll bring you your change with the pyjamas.'

Waiting, I stared from the tiny window at the multiplicity of lights reaching to an invisible horizon. Here and there a taller building soared glowing from the firmament. Below, in a street hidden from my view, a vehicle huffed and snorted, evidently manoeuvring into a tight space; as it came to rest, other traffic revved its motors, gathered pace in a united roar. Above, something winked, catching my eye. The red pulsing light of an aircraft, drifting invisibly across the night sky. I was following its course when the door-catch plinked behind me.

'Found you an old toothbrush as well,' she announced. 'Just in case you need one.'

'That is kind.'

'Breakfast from eight-thirty. Hope you sleep well.' She took a final glance around the room. 'Good night.'

'Good night, and thank you.'

When her footfalls had died on the staircase I closed

the door and shot the bolt.

Something aroused me.

Reaching out for the bedside lamp, I knocked it to the carpet. The muted thud added itself to the other noises in my brain, creating an impression of uproar. For a while I lay still, waiting for questioning voices outside. Nothing came.

Releasing myself cautiously from the bedclothes, I groped around the floor until the lamp came into my grasp; the bulb still answered to the switch. My watch told me it was two-fifteen.

Treading over to the door, I stood listening. Somewhere there was a faint creaking. A night breeze had got up: that could have accounted for the sound. Was this what had disturbed me?

I slid back the bolt. The door opened with a soprano squeal of hinges to which a clatter from the window-fastener responded as a through-draught was created. From the doorway I peered down the stairs.

A ruby-coloured night-bulb illuminated them dimly, its light only just reaching the bottom where a fire-door led on to the third-floor landing. After some hesitation I began the descent, selecting places for my bare feet on the thin carpeting.

At the halfway stage I was overtaken by giddiness. Gripping the handrail for support, I heard noises again. They seemed to have no exterior source: they came from inside my brain. Valerie's startled voice. *I don't think he meant any harm. Confused, isn't he? Let him go.* Plus a babble of other sounds. Barbara's sleepy treble: *Hallo, Daddy . . .* The final thump of Elkins's body, hitting the foot of the stairs; the angle of his head . . .

Out of the gloom came a sustained moan. My fingers

were tight upon the curved rail; by relaxing them, I
knew, I should plunge the rest of the way, helpless against
vertigo. I waited for the moaning to stop. Vaguely I
sensed that its cessation rested with me: it was my res-
ponsibility. From this it was a long stride across a yawning
gulf to the realization that it came from my own throat.
When awareness did struggle through, I sat on the staircase and commenced some ritualistic deep breathing to
restore order to my mental processes, allowing myself
time.

Finally I was able to pull myself back to the attic and
shut the door. Securing it with the bolt, I left the lamp
switched on and returned to bed, lying on my back to
contemplate the blankness of the ceiling so that my mind
could accommodate the thoughts and images and recollections that I knew were mustering for an assault.

CHAPTER 7

Unless we had laughed, our wedding day would have been
more than the disaster it was.

To avoid mishap we had agreed upon register office and
immediate relatives only. Somehow, in the insidious
manner of such events, inflation occurred: it became a
gathering of forty and a hotel reception at which Valerie's
mother arrived in hysterical ruins after tripping into a
puddle in the car park. The favourite uncle who was to
propose the happy couple had spent lunchtime bracing
himself conscientiously for the ordeal with the aid of a
bottle, achieving a state of incoherent aggressiveness
surpassed only by that of my own father, who had conceived a pathological dislike of Valerie's family in it

entirety and devoted his afternoon to the fomenting of factional jealousies. On the insertion of a knife, the cake collapsed into pieces. The small son of Valerie's elder sister emptied a strawberry jelly in the centre of the polished floor, to the subsequent detriment of my least favourite aunt in the course of a hurried exit in search of the powder room . . .

That night we laughed, Valerie and I, uncontrollably, as we lived in retrospect the celebratory shambles. We agreed that we wouldn't have missed it for worlds.

Two days later our honeymoon was over. I had to sit for some intermediate exams, while Valerie had exhausted her holiday entitlement and was due back at a Government desk. 'What a relief,' she remarked, 'to return to normal.'

I said, 'When our daughter gets married – if matrimony still exists by then – I suggest we do her a real favour by disregarding the whole thing.'

'I don't know,' Valerie said thoughtfully. 'I'd hate to cheat her out of a good chuckle.'

A year later we moved into a small house at Purley. By this time Valerie was expecting Barbara and had left her job; I had qualified and been promoted. Metallurgy was my speciality. The people with whom I worked advised me that I could earn more by going into industry, but something told me to remain for the time being under the State umbrella; and in fact, a firm that I had seriously considered joining went into liquidation a few months later and its facilities were nationalized. I stayed with the Government research institute at Mitcham while continuing to look around.

Barbara arrived. The Purley house appeared to undergo shrinkage. We moved again, this time to North London, because the laboratories had been transferred to an elderly warehouse in the King's Cross area. The new house stood in its own ground and boasted enough space to enable us to cope with the arrival, three and a half years after his sister, of Michael.

There was difficulty with Michael. At five months he developed, or revealed, an obscure muscular defect which put him into hospital; for a year afterwards he needed special care at home, and this had to come mainly from Valerie, who rose staunchly to the challenge while I chased my career from the Government warehouse to Kaltmans. This was a company which in my view had a future and moreover was concerned with the type of research that held most fascination for me: the behaviour of metals under the most extreme conditions. Here I was happy. The head of my department, Melville Simpson, was a man in his early fifties whose faintly supercilious air concealed an acute and sympathetic mind: we were immediately in rapport, and before long I was given virtually a free hand to develop my own lines of investigation with the help of an assistant, in collaboration with whom I published my first paper in *Science Focus*. It brought me some correspondence. I addressed a scientific conference or two, gained the ears of a number of learned contemporaries including Walter Brent, that toiling author of a timeless textbook; and was asked to contribute a second thesis. It brought me also a minor personal crisis.

Its name was Sally, and she was my assistant. Sally Masters, with an honours degree in physics from Cambridge and a fetching way of wrinkling her nose. A sound worker, a good listener, and no overt propensity towards Women's Lib. At the time when we were working on the first paper, Valerie at home had been coping with Michael's particular needs for eight months, and the effort was tiring her out. For a while, the Kaltmans atmosphere was a lot livelier than that at Birch Holme, The Park, Finchley. I would arrive home to siege conditions, feel obliged to help out, and have to provide solace and sustenance for an exhausted wife during a period when – I sought to convince myself – I had some entitlement to a little of the same for myself.

I began to work late on two evenings a week. Sally agreed to adjust her hours accordingly. It was all in the cause of research.

This went on for a month or two. After each spell of overtime Sally and I would eat out together, just a drink and sandwiches, and laugh a good deal. Once, instead of working, we went to a cinema. Well-merited relaxation therapy, I expounded: we should work the better for it afterwards. On two occasions I took her home, and on the second of them she invited me in for a scotch. I stayed longer than I had planned.

At Kaltmans our relationship remained outwardly a professional one. If anything, my attitude towards her was cooler than it might have been to a male associate; but at some time during the second month I had become aware that in unguarded moments the eyes I was thinking of were violet rather than hazel, and suddenly I was worried. The second paper for *Science Focus* was by then almost complete. Taking Sally aside, I told her it was time to ease up and that further overtime would be unnecessary. She got the message.

'It's been fun, John,' she said demurely. Her voice was engagingly cracked when it pitched on certain notes. 'I've really enjoyed the work. Don't hesitate to ask again, should the need arise.'

'For the time being,' I said, more curtly than I had intended, 'I don't plan to produce any more papers. It's not fair on Val.'

'Of course not,' she agreed at once, 'Having a sticky time, isn't she? She'll be glad to see more of you, I expect.'

The ease of it filled me with relief. In the laboratory our professional alliance remained undamaged, but on the other level I had backed off and nothing more needed to be said. Sally began to go around with an accountant from the admin section; I started getting home earlier. Michael made rapid strides. The burden on Valerie lifted. Now and then we felt able to entrust the children to a babysitter and go out for a quiet meal. The situation had stabilized.

To the best of my knowledge, Valerie had never had cause for a moment's doubt. She barely knew I had a female assistant, and in any case, I reminded myself, my dalliance with Sally had endured for too brief a time for major complications to arise. Apart from which, my basic affection for Valerie had remained unshaken. Sally had been around at an unfortunate time, that was all. I was glad to have taken action when I did.

A year after this I was at something of a dead end.

Kaltmans had moved to modern premises in Kilburn: we had up-to-date facilities and a famine of projects. As ever, the economic climate was to blame. Schemes for high-speed transport and the development of new industrial machinery were in abeyance, which meant that we were starved of commitments. Although we prided ourselves on our versatility, a high proportion of our work was in this field, and anything bad for the manufacturers was terrible for us. Towards the end of an especially trying week that had seen the suspension, if not the demise, of at least three promising programmes, I was called into Mel Simpson's office.

'Nothing urgent on, have you, John?'

I gave him the crooked smile I kept for cynical moments. 'How does it look?'

'That's exactly how it looks. The reason I ask . . .'

He tapped his front teeth with the end of a wooden ruler. I hated the way he did that. To distract him I said, 'You want me to update the files on Accelerator and Headway?' – the two major undertakings that had lately taken a back seat. There was a boyish streak to Simpson that delighted in project-names more appropriate to space missions.

'Christ, no,' he said warmly. 'That's an admin job for someone, keep 'em out of mischief. What I wanted to ask you . . .' Again he hesitated.

'Is whether,' I suggested, 'I'd be willing to go out and rob a bullion van of a million or two?'

'We're not bankrupt yet. Not cashwise, anyhow. The commodity we're short of . . .' The ruler finalized its dental explorations with a xylophonic run. 'As you know, John, up to now we've tended to give Government work the cold shoulder: too fond of our independence.' He paused, conning the ruler markings. 'But there does come a time when one has to rethink in the light of circumstances, and the bald fact is – '

'That schemes underwritten by the taxpayer are more reliable.'

He shrugged. 'One must be steered by realities.'

I sat back in my chair of padded plastic hide and stainless steel. 'So what's the proposition?'

'A Service contract,' he said bluntly.

'Breaking new ground for us, isn't it?'

'Not entirely. We can hardly pretend that some of our past work hasn't had military applications, if that's what somebody liked to use it for. And obviously somebody did. We'd be very naïve to blink the fact. There's only a shade of difference between that and a direct commitment to – '

'There's a world of difference,' I said.

He regarded me speculatively. 'I know your feelings on this, John. Why do you think I'm creeping up on it like a fox on a lamb? I don't like it much more than you do. But as I say, I believe one has to face a situation as it stands: and the current situation is that without projects to work on, Kaltmans goes out of business. That means you, me, all of us. A host of talent scattered to the winds. If that happened – '

'We'd all find something.'

'Would we? Well, maybe. But where? In a Whitehall establishment, likely as not, without a choice between military and civil programmes.'

'Do we have a choice now?' I asked.

'Not at this precise moment. But if we can just ride it out, get by without actual State support – '

'What's a military contract,' I countered, 'if it's not State support?'

He gestured with a sad smile. 'Okay. I admit it's all figures of speech, verbal gymnastics, call it what you like. The fact remains, if we can survive this period there's a fighting chance of Kaltmans keeping its identity for the time when things get better . . . I think we all want this, don't we?'

I got up and strolled to the window. From there I said, 'I think you're putting it to me as a straight loyalty issue. Personal principles versus corporate survival.'

'Maybe I am.'

I turned. 'Don't principles mean that much?'

'To me? Yes, they mean a hell of a lot. But what principles are we talking about?'

'I only have the one set.'

'Which could be where you slip up,' he said drily.

'Principles aren't divisible . . . to use the modern jargon.'

Simpson shone me a comprehending smile. 'In the abstract, John, it's a glorious philosophy. In the concrete it tends to crumble. I always think of that wretched old woman in the Dickens novel, forever bewailing the miseries of the African natives while her own children starved on her doorstep.'

'That was priorities, not principles.'

'And that, if you'll permit me, is more semantics. Anyhow,' he added more briskly, 'I just thought I'd make the overtures this morning and leave you to contemplate the echoes. There's no blinding rush. We have till the end of the month.' He pulled a folder towards him.

On my way to the door I paused. 'Why me, anyway? Couldn't you take the contract and put Doug Clark in charge? Or Frank Selby?'

Laughter exploded briefly from Simpson. 'That'd make it all right, would it, John? You could square that with your conscience?' He said it kindly. 'If you want to know, you've been specifically asked for. They want someone with scientific flair allied to creative imagination and they seem to think you've got both. Go away and think about it.' He went into a slouch over the folder as though examining it for hairline cracks.

I discussed the matter with Valerie.

She saw things much as I did, with the addition of a healthy dash of feminine realism. 'After all,' she argued, 'suppose Doug Clark, for instance, took it on instead of you . . . would you quit Kaltmans?'

'No. No, I wouldn't.'

'Why not?'

I gazed at her. 'Because my work's there, I suppose. It's what I love to do.'

'So for this reason you want Kaltmans to keep going?'

'Naturally.'

'So as long as someone else does the dirty work . . .'

'I don't think that's altogether fair.'

Michael began calling out upstairs. When Valerie returned from attending to him, I said, 'I see what you're getting at. I'd be making use of the soiled money, just like everyone else in the outfit.'

'If you regard it as soiled.'

I gestured despairingly. 'I loathe anything to do with war. But Mel Simpson's right, possibly – how do you divorce one thing from another in an age like this?'

'You can't.' Valerie took up the sock she was darning. 'You can only come to a decision on relative merits.'

'Compromise.' I threw the evening newspaper away. 'There ought to be a way of getting through life without this eternal coming to terms, teetering halfway to meet some phoney requirement – '

'I agree; but there isn't. Strictly speaking, someone like you should refuse to pay taxes because part of them help pay for the war machine . . .'

'Some people do refuse.'

'And end up as idiotic martyrs with bees in their bonnets: they don't *achieve* anything. You can do better than that. By helping to keep Kaltmans in business you could be paving the way for a later discovery that could result in . . . improved kidney machines or something.' Valerie looked up earnestly from the sock. 'You have to weigh these things.'

'I know I do.' I meditated. 'I'll talk to Mel again in

the morning,' I said finally.

I took on the job. My sole stipulation was that Sally should be my number one; we worked well together, she had ideas to contribute, and I felt that the situation between us was well enough in hand to be discounted. Douglas Clark, a contemporary of mine, was brilliant in his way; but we clashed. My private opinion of Frank Selby was that he was reasonably sound but infuriatingly slow. Both of them were co-opted on to my team, as we needed all the strength we could muster, but each was given, in deference to his seniority, a freer-ranging role than the others.

Of my own capacity I had few doubts. My detached, impartial judgement of myself, painstakingly formed over the years, clashed in no major respect with that of the Defence Ministry experts who, according to Simpson, had requested my services. It was not vanity. If a cricketer scores a century against fine bowling on a sticky wicket, he can accept with perfect confidence selection for the next Test. Once my initial scruples were overcome I threw myself with energy into the project, not doubting our ability to carry it through without undue loss of time.

Things, however, went rather badly.

In the first place, my choice of a team proved far from ideal. Some of its male components resented the presence of a woman, however gifted, as second in command, and spent as much time trying to upstage her as working constructively. This had its effect upon Sally, who became over-anxious. She wanted to prove herself, and so she tried short cuts that in other circumstances she would have had the patience to shun. Several times we had to halt and start again.

Secondly, scouts from the Ministry kept arriving to see how we were getting on. They were like pests buzzing

around our collars. They said little, except in confidence
to Simpson, who later passed abridged versions on to us
in a well-meaning bid for industrial peace which failed
to convince us that the Ministry men were not becoming
steadily more querulous. Judging by what Simpson let
slip, they were obsessed with the cost factor: a major
scandal over Government expenditure had only recently
been glossed over, and the activities of the Ombudsman
had acquired new menace. At the same time, the speci-
fications to which we were supposed to be working were
constantly being revised, sometimes quite drastically.
Any one of these 'minor' alterations could nullify a
fortnight's work at the stroke of a pen.

The brickbats fell on me. As project manager I didn't
complain: if we achieved success, applause would come
my way in similar amounts: nevertheless it all added to
the strain. What was worse, whispers began to circulate
that I had chosen Sally as my deputy for personal reasons.

This was damaging. The more so, since there had
been a time when such an insinuation might have con-
tained more than an element of truth. The fact that Sally
was now lustily involved with – among others – a physical
education instructor at a further education establishment
in Hampstead was of small account; she was the type to
whom mud of almost any consistency will readily adhere;
and yet the whispers were not penetrating enough to
justify my shouting them down. They simply drifted
gently about the place, making the atmosphere slightly
toxic. My fear was that they might travel further. Valerie
would, of course, ignore them; but they could be upsetting.

To depose Sally in favour of someone else was not a
solution. Unless she had proved incompetent, it would
have been too obvious; and she was not incompetent. Or
if she was, so were we all.

I explained this to Simpson, to whom I took all my problems. 'We're like a squad of rookies,' I told him, 'undergoing military drill. No one's to blame, in particular. It's just a different ball game as far as we're concerned, and we're still learning the rules.'

A practical man, he winced at the metaphor. 'Stick with it,' he advised.

'Will the Ministry stick with us?'

'They've not said otherwise.'

'I can't understand why they haven't shifted the work to one of their own establishments.'

'Perhaps,' he suggested, 'you're not doing as badly as you imagine. No doubt they're well used to these setbacks.'

'If so, no wonder my taxes keep going up.'

It was his turn for a stroll to the window. He stared across the wire-encircled compound to the main road with its polluting juggernauts transmitting an endless thudding hum. 'How far,' he said eventually, 'are you from any sort of a breakthrough?'

I took my time.

'Haven't a clue,' I replied.

His spine remained rigid. 'Still toiling entirely in the dark?'

'You've got to remember, so far we've been given at least five different operational requirements, which means – '

'I've not forgotten. And for our part I think we have to bear in mind that in defence work this is inevitable. We're new to it: it hits us hard. We're used to plodding from A to B, pausing for a little profit, then trudging on to C. Service needs are more . . . fluid. In this field especially. Near as I can make out, tank warfare changes all the time. The emphasis is switching to counter-measures – which to me makes sense.'

'It may make sense,' I said, 'but it also makes difficulties. They want a launcher that a man can virtually pack
into his haversack. All right. They also want it with
enough beef to blast apart a battle-tank at four thousand
yards . . . eight thousand, probably, by Monday. There's
no known material that can – '

Simpson swung about. 'No *known* material,' he repeated. 'That's what this is all about, isn't it?'

'My point is, the Ministry bloodhounds should make
allowances for the fact that we're turning up new soil.'

'I'm sure they do. Isn't this why they haven't taken
the contract away?'

I was silent. Simpson returned from the window to
rest a hand on my shoulder. 'Relax, John. You'll all work
better if you do.'

'I wish I could believe that.'

Reoccupying his chair, he gave me a sharp glance.
'Complaints?'

'Oh, nothing serious.'

'But something,' he insisted.

'Trifling lack of lubrication here and there. Trivial.'

'The effect might not be. What's the cause?'

'This and that. I think I might have made a mistake
in choosing Sally.'

His bright gaze rested upon mine. 'How come?'

'Some of them resent her.'

'But she's always been your number one.'

'Not in a combined project, though.'

He nodded slowly. 'I get it. Collective male ego in
jeopardy.' Having mused for a few moments, he looked
across once more. 'I wondered if you were referring to
something else.'

'Such as what?'

He prevaricated. 'Something more delicate.'

'To do with Sally, you mean?'

'I was on the wrong track . . . forget it. The great thing,' he said with a show of heartiness, 'is for you to push on in the knowledge that your particular problems are understood. Don't try to break time records. Just keep digging.'

CHAPTER 8

Obviously the whisper had reached Simpson. In his over-subtle way he had probed before pulling back, offering me the chance to say something, deny something; then had withdrawn altogether, no doubt thankful to be spared embarrassment. But it was a warning. If Simpson had heard mutterings, they were becoming too fortissimo for comfort. I decided upon attack.

I took Sally home for dinner.

As I had hoped, she and Valerie hit it off admirably. I had made it a practice to speak of Sally now and then: not too much: enough to familiarize Valerie with her existence and make a dinner invitation a reasonably natural event. It was, I explained, to mark a possible turning-point in our work on the project. As though divining my purpose, Sally dressed plainly, arranged her hair unbecomingly and held the conversation throughout to an academic level. Valerie kept her end up well, helped by her Civil Service experience. They were charmed with one another. At a moderate hour we drove Sally to the Tube station, Valerie urging her to repeat the visit. On the way home she said, 'What a nice person she is.'

'Sally? Yes, we get on all right. Her work tends to be

a bit slapdash at times.'

'I mean personally nice, you automaton. Don't you ever stop thinking of your work?'

'Yes. Every Tuesday.'

'Tuesday? What's special about Tuesday?'

'When you wash your hair. For an hour or two I don't recognize you in those rollers, so I worry, so I forget work.'

'Idiot.'

After this I relaxed a little. Sally was an accepted identity in the household instead of an unseen presence about whom there could be murmurs. A certain amount of feeling remained detectable in the ranks of my team at Kaltmans, but by now the work was going somewhat better and the general mood had improved. Although everybody knew it was a defence contract, only four of us knew precisely what the end product was intended to be: myself, Sally, Frank Selby – whose stolid dependability had turned out to be an asset – and an older man, Tony Phillison, who had been with Kaltmans for years. Each of us had been security screened. Our clearances seemed to have involved remarkably little, but I supposed that the Special Branch, or whoever was responsible, knew what they were doing. Anyhow, as I remarked to Sally, by the time we produced anything worth developing it would be obsolete, so what did it matter?

She frowned. 'I'm not so sure.'

'Sure of what?'

'The unimportance you seem to attach to secrecy. Other countries could be interested in this, couldn't they?'

'They've got their own teams hard at it, don't you worry.'

'But suppose they're not as far advanced as us?'

My laughter made a vulgar noise. 'Then all I can say is, the world of science is crammed tighter with incompetent twits than I'd previously imagined.'

She remained serious. 'I still think you take it too lightly. We're on classified work: any of us could easily be at risk.'

The idea was novel enough to pull me up. I considered it for a moment.

'No one's told me to carry a gun or avoid the shadows.'

'Nobody wants melodrama. But there's no harm in taking a few precautions.'

'Do you?' I asked curiously.

'I don't walk by myself in lonely spots, if that's what you mean. And I bolt my door at night.'

'Sensible measures at the best of times.'

'But this is beside the point,' she said, studying a graph above her workbench. 'My real argument was, any one of us knows enough about this project to be of use to a rival set-up if he liked to hawk it around.'

'I notice you say he.'

'For convenience only.' There was in fact one other female in the team, a woman in her late forties called Joan Petworth; relatively a passenger, but useful for odd bursts of eccentric inspiration which once in a blue moon led somewhere. 'I don't think you can rule anyone out.'

'Even me?' I suggested.

'You especially. You could blow the lot.'

'Thanks. There's not much to blow at the moment.'

But it set me thinking. If such a thing had occurred to Sally it could occur to anyone. My own ingenuousness, I now saw, had been a little startling. I had regarded my screening lightheartedly, almost flippantly: the profounder implications had escaped me. Before we embarked, Mel Simpson had read us a modified Riot Act relating to

unguarded tongues, and there had been a printed notice
for each of us from the Ministry; but much of my previous
work in the commercial sphere had been subject to similar
constraints and I had come to think nothing of them.
After my talk with Sally I pondered more deeply. Then
I spoke to Simpson.

'Just assuming one of us had an approach of some kind
from another source: what's the procedure?'

'Stall,' he replied promptly. 'Then let me know.'

'What would you do?'

'Notify the authorities.'

'That has a pleasantly vague ring to it.' I surveyed him
reflectively. 'Might some danger be involved?'

He gave me a hard look in return. 'Who to?'

'The person approached.'

'Only if he were stupid enough to fall for the bait.
Anyone like that among your bunch?'

'I wouldn't think so.'

'Don't you know?'

'I don't see how anyone can be certain.'

His expression softened to one of indulgence. 'I told
them,' he remarked, 'you were just the man for the job.
The archetypal brilliant scientist with a simple worldly
outlook. It may interest you to know, John, that each
and every one of your team – yourself included – has been
investigated so thoroughly that the security boys know
more about them and their connections than they probably
know themselves. All right, there are no certainties . . .
but this is about as near as you can get.'

I digested the information. 'People's circumstances
change,' I ventured.

'Sure. That's why there's continued surveillance of
the lot of you.'

I felt a nudge of anger. 'It's a bloody intrusion.'

'You were all given a strong hint of the system,' he pointed out.

His earlier words had riled me. 'Simple I may be, but couldn't there be danger in that too? Other factions might trade on my simplicity to convince me I'd be doing mankind a favour by spreading knowledge around.'

'Oh, it's happened.'

'So what's the Service doing about it?'

'Keeping a fond eye on you.'

'How?'

'I'm afraid that's their business. Look, John,' said Simpson, appearing vexed with himself, 'I didn't mean to say all this, only I thought you were due for some sensible answers and, as you know, I've total faith in you. None of it signifies a row of beans. It's routine. All you have to worry about – '

'Is delivering the goods. That's worry enough to be going on with.'

'Still blocked?'

'Let's say we're continuing to plane through a knot in the wood. Every so often a chunk gets bitten off, but what's left underneath is pretty rough.'

'Fond of your metaphors, aren't you? You're a bit of a rarity,' he said on a shrewd note, tapping his desk with the end of a pencil. 'A research man with a genuine creative imagination. You can go far, provided you keep it harnessed.'

'I'll try not to get carried away,' I said. 'At present things aren't going smoothly enough to give me big ideas.'

'You'll get there.'

'And when we do?' I looked at him searchingly. 'Does Kaltmans then get back to legitimate industrial assignments? Or are we mysteriously committed to the military for the rest of time?'

He shook an emphatic head. 'Over my dead body.'

'What we need,' I said, rising, 'is a Breakthrough. One of the kind that pitch the Press into convulsions for three days running. Then we could hand this thing over to the development boys and get everybody off our backs.'

'Fine idea,' he agreed blandly. 'See what you can manage.'

That evening Valerie looked troubled.

A man had called, she explained, claiming to be from the council's rating department and asking for permission to take some measurements around the house. Valerie at the time had her hands full with Michael, who was in an awkward mood: she was also mixing a cake. Without taking too much notice of the man she told him to go ahead.

Five minutes later, remembering his existence, she walked round to the back of the house to find him leaning against the glazed door that connected the living-room with the patio. Exactly what he was doing, she couldn't describe. At her approach he moved away and began to fuss around with a tape measure that lay along the flagstones – rather as though it had been placed there as a blind. 'His manner gave me the creeps,' she said with a shiver. 'I can't tell you why. The way he was leaning on that door . . . I don't think he expected me to come round from the kitchen as quietly as I did. I was wearing my felt slippers.'

'Did he say anything?'

'Some drivel about getting the tape to lie flat and didn't we have a pleasant outlook. I was a bit short with him, deliberately.'

'How much longer did he stick around?'

'He left soon after. I watched from the window and

saw him take off in a car.'

'Take off?'

'Yes. He didn't call at any of the other houses. Just drove away towards the main road.'

'Was it an official-looking car?'

'Ordinary saloon – Renault, I think.'

After a period of cogitation I said, 'Tomorrow I'll phone the Town Hall – '

'I've done that. Someone in the rates department said their inspectors did go round taking measurements, but he couldn't say whether our address would have been on anyone's list for today. Said he'd make inquiries. Of course I've not heard another word.'

I poured each of us a medium-dry sherry. It was our moment of relaxation before dinner. A drawing of Michael's lay on the table; I picked it up. 'Mummy?' I queried. 'Daddy? The Creature from Galaxy Seven?' For a moment I studied the bulbous outlines. 'I expect he was from the Town Hall all right.'

'Then he should confine himself to his job,' said Valerie. She sounded unconvinced.

The Breakthrough arrived a week later.

Like so many things of the kind, it stole up practically unannounced. The erratic Joan Petworth was the first to spot its significance; quite casually she pointed it out to Frank Selby, who came to me in some excitement and said, enunciating carefully, that he could be wrong but there was a possibility we might be on to something.

He wasn't wrong. None of us was wrong. We had been on the right lines for weeks: it had just needed a final shunt. The new material, the wonder-alloy that cleared the way to everything else, was there for the taking. We stood around breaking open cans of beer and laughing with slight hysteria. Then I reported to Simpson.

'Great stuff, John,' he said, permitting himself a
moment's extravagance. 'You're quite certain?'

'The formula's watertight: we're all agreed on that.
It'll do what's asked of it.'

'But it's got to have trials.'

'Yes, of course. Frank can supervise those.'

'While you return thankfully to Accelerator or Headway? I don't know, John.' Picking up the ruler, he bared
his teeth. 'I think you should see the project out of the
building.'

I uttered a groan. 'If you say so. I was hoping – '

'I know you were.' The ruler scuttled along the enamel.
'You've had a bellyful and I don't blame you. But until
this thing is thoroughly tested we've not fulfilled the contract, and you're part of the contract.'

I lifted my arms. 'Okay.'

'And I don't need to emphasize,' he added, 'the security
aspect. Now it's more vital than ever.'

It seemed a propitious time to have Sally home to
dinner again. To lay the ghost more comprehensively, I
invited Frank Selby also; and after some hesitation, Tony
Phillison. Neither of them was an obvious choice of guest,
except that with Sally they had been my senior colleagues
on the project and the dinner was ostensibly to celebrate
its success.

This time things went less well.

To begin with, Sally turned up looking the complete
sexpot in a flared and diaphanous outfit that would have
turned heads at St Tropez; presumably she reasoned
that with two other males present it was not incumbent
upon her to repeat her previous performance of total
sobriety, but as she entered the house I saw Valerie's
eyes widen. Frank Selby, who had brought Sally in his

car, was evidently knocked out by her, and barely uttered.
This left Phillison, whose taciturnity was a legend at the
firm. He seemed to spend all his waking hours solving
equations in his head, and it was soon manifest that a
dinner-party was not going to be allowed to interfere
with the habit.

The upshot was that Sally, who was in festive mood,
felt obliged to enlist me as her sole ally in some cross-
table banter that on another occasion might have been
harmless. Selby, after some sporadic attempts to compete,
retired into a moody silence. Phillison was in any case a
write-off. Valerie had tried half-heartedly and in vain to
open him up over the vermouth, and she now abandoned
the task, leaving Sally and me in verbal control. Short of
allowing the meal to proceed in a dumb stillness, I had
no alternative but to play along.

I cursed the impulse that had made me invite them.
I wished I had included Simpson: always first-rate
company in a social setting. Even Joan Petworth would
have been an improvement on Phillison. She and Valerie
could have chatted. But the damage was done: I was
trapped in the last situation I had wanted or allowed for –
vocal exchanges with a sparkling Sally in front of a silent
wife, whose smile grew tighter as the night advanced.

Luckily, Phillison had to leave in good time. No doubt
he had some unfinished equations waiting at home. His
departure gave Selby the cue, twenty minutes later, to
whisk Sally away. By then her manner could only be
described as catastrophic. If she was conscious of the
effect she was having, she didn't care. Her parting comment was: 'See you tomorrow, John . . . usual time.' It
wasn't the words; it was the way she said them. Her white
arm waved from the car as it roared off. Never had I
watched the rear of a vehicle with a more enormous

sense of deliverance. My head was buzzing as I walked back into the house.

'My God,' I said, collecting bottles, 'I'm not sorry that's over.'

Valerie, who had been straightening furniture, picked up a brimming ashtray and took it to the kitchen. I followed.

'That guy Phillison,' I remarked, running hot water over dishes. 'The original blight, isn't he? Sorry about that. I never realized.'

'I'll do those,' she said briefly, coming to the sink.

I stood aside. 'We won't have them again. That's a promise.'

'Doesn't matter,' she said indifferently.

'Yes, it does. You hated it, I could see.'

'It didn't bother me. One way or another.'

Sensing the cliff-edge, I retreated to the living-room to sit with the evening paper in a pretence of relaxation. Washing-up noises came from the kitchen for some time. At last they abated. I altered my grip on the newsprint, ready to cast it at the first excuse. She appeared at the doorway.

'I'm very tired. I'm going to bed.'

Before I could reply she was gone. I made a show to myself of reading some more, then followed her up. My intention had been to voice some humorous nothings as I undressed, but she seemed to be in a sound sleep.

At breakfast the next morning she was much pre-occupied by the children, both of whom were in rumbustious form. There was no chance of a quiet word. At the time I was due to leave she was busy with Michael in the bathroom: I called, 'Cheerio – back early' through the locked door, listened for a reply that didn't come, and left the house with a weight in my stomach, cursing impulse with renewed vigour.

Frank Selby was alone in the laboratory when I arrived. His answer to my greeting was morose. I said, 'Trust we didn't ply you with too much plonk.'

'It was very good,' he said with such manifest hypocrisy that I cringed for him. After a heavy pause he added, 'Sally clearly enjoyed it.'

'Must have been the company.'

'One member of it, anyway,' he said spitefully. Having said this, he couldn't resist going on. 'What's the secret, John? What's your way with the ladies?'

'Make free with the cut-price Spanish.' I smiled, but I could have slaughtered him where he stood. His resentment hung about him like autumn mist, and I knew he would talk.

The moment Sally put in an appearance, I took her aside. 'You really gummed things up last night.'

'Me?' She was genuinely astonished. 'What do you mean?'

'All that arch business bouncing between the two of us . . . why the hell didn't you talk to the others?'

'Because,' she retorted, not unreasonably, 'they didn't seem inclined to talk back.' Her eyes darted fire. 'Good God, I thought I was helping out. Why did you play along if it was a funeral supper you wanted?'

The fact that she was partly right did nothing to soothe me. 'Valerie and I aren't speaking. Lord knows what ideas you gave her.'

'I gave her?'

Sally's voice had soared, drawing glances from distant parts of the laboratory. She ignored my frantic gestures. 'Any ideas she gets are her own. Don't drag me into it.'

'All right,' I muttered, waving her down. Her words had carried. I spotted an exchange of malicious smiles between Paul Chappell, the team's youngest and slimiest member, and the ubiquitous Joan Petworth, whose right ear, somebody had once observed, was trumpet-shaped for the reception of choice morsels. 'Let's just forget it, shall we?'

'I'd no wish to be reminded in the first place,' she said clearly, walking off.

It speedily became apparent to me that I was in bad odour on all sides, with Frank Selby for having been invited and with most of the others for not having been invited. My modest dinner party was beginning to achieve the dimensions of a major diplomatic gaffe. Only Phillison seemed equable. After a terse 'Thanks for a pleasant evening, Tiverton' he got on with the day's work inside his habitual cocoon of placidity, the eye at the centre of the hurricane. I turned to the refuge of my own activities, hoping the thing would blow over.

To an extent it did. But relations with Frank Selby had undergone distortion; and with Sally I was now on a new and less happy footing. Neither eventuality broke my heart, but I was glad that the end of the project was in sight. When it was reached, I intended to ask Simpson for a solo assignment: I was a little tired of coping with temperaments.

In the meantime, there was Valerie.

On reaching home that evening I found the house silent. A note on the kitchen table informed me that she had taken the children to a tea-party at Gillian's from which they would not return until eight. Having gnawed at the beef salad left beneath Polythene wraps, I watched a television comedy half-hour without hearing or seeing a thing, and then fell into a doze. I had a dream.

A man was trying to get through the french door. One immense hand was pushing at the framework, bending it inwards; although his face was in shadow, somehow I knew he was grinning. The glass of the door was making cracking sounds. Trying to rise from the chair, I found myself locked in place. The man outside was not alone. Behind him in the darkness were others, waiting for the yielding of the door to surge forward. I fought to call out. Nothing got past the base of my throat. I struggled. From somewhere came the ripple of a laugh . . .

The children were in the room with me, excitedly full of the tea-party. They danced and chattered while I pulled myself together, feeling terrible. From the doorway Valerie surveyed me coolly; I had the feeling – perhaps it was wishful – that a moment earlier she had been watching with some concern as I strained and gasped in my sleep. If she had, there was no sign of it as she said briskly, 'Michael, you must go to bed immediately,' and whisked him away. She was back in the haven of child-care: there was no way through to her. I read Barbara a good-night story, giving it a tenth of my attention while the bulk of my mind stayed with the problem.

To me, this was a new Valerie. I had never deemed her capable of a 'mood' lasting above twenty minutes; but then I had never hurt her before. What was the treatment? I was in the position of having to feel my way, devise soothing ointments without practice in the relevant branch of chemistry. While she was putting Barbara to bed I made coffee, arranged it with biscuits and the evening newspaper beside her favourite chair, and ensured that the room was neat. Feeling stupid, I tested the french door and found it secure. Light from the room lit up the patio, displaying its emptiness. For a few seconds I stared out, trying to smile at the vestiges of the dream, before returning to my chair to wait.

I heard Valerie return from upstairs and go into the

kitchen. A considerable period elapsed. At last I joined her there.

'Coffee's getting cold.'

She pulled a slight face. 'Coffee? Couldn't touch it.' She was ironing small garments. 'Gillian gave us more than enough.' She pressed a pleat, giving it much concentration.

'Bit of a junior bunfight, was it?'

'Just a tea-party.' She began on another pleat.

This seemed to provide an opening. 'Speaking of parties,' I said, 'last night wasn't exactly – '

'There's no need to maul it over.'

There was a perilous lilt to her voice. A new Valerie indeed. I stood back, giving her room as she moved round to attack the pleat from the other end.

'I wasn't planning to maul anything. But I think I owe you an explanation. The reason I – '

'There's nothing that needs explaining.' A smudge of brown appeared on the skirt. 'Damn,' she said, dusting it with the back of her fingers.

'An apology, then. It was a bloody terrible evening and I shouldn't have inflicted it on you.'

'There I agree,' she said after a pause. 'You should have kept it tête-à-tête.'

'What does that mean?' I asked unwisely.

'Well, you could have done without the two male stooges, I should have thought.'

'You'd have preferred Sally by herself?'

'You would, I'm sure.'

Folding the skirt, she added it to the ironed pile and took up a blouse.

'That,' I said quietly, 'was uncalled for.'

'I don't invariably wait for a call. Don't forget your coffee.'

'To hell with the coffee. I made it for both of us, hoping we might have a quiet talk . . . but you seem determined to take the sourest view of everything at the moment. Look,' I went on, getting heated, 'I fixed up last night in good faith as a gesture to my three main colleagues, and since you and Sally seemed to get on so well the time before – '

'I shouldn't judge by appearances.' The blouse was in place on the ironing board; she went at it with short, energetic strokes.

'That's precisely what you seem to be doing. Sally's not like that, you know.'

'Like what?'

'She was behaving out of character.'

'Oh? You know a lot about her character?'

I sat on the end of the board, arresting her arm as it came forward with the iron. She made no effort to withdraw. She merely froze, staring down at the blouse as though analysing the weave.

'We may as well cut out all the innuendo,' I suggested. 'In plain terms, you're saying I made a fool of myself with Sally last night and you didn't appreciate having to watch. That close enough?'

'Not bang on target,' she said in a low voice.

'What, then?'

'But it'll do, I suppose.' She gave me a flicker of a glance. 'I hated it, John.'

'I know, love.' It was like being washed ashore after a storm. 'I wasn't too happy myself. But if she and I hadn't gone into a routine, we'd have eaten in total silence.'

'How do you know?' She took a quick breath and hurried on. 'But it doesn't matter. I understand . . . I think I do . . . and it's an idiotic thing to quarrel about.' Her face came up, this time to stay. I kissed her nose. She gave a small tremulous laugh. 'That coffee stone cold, should you think?'

'A lab man,' I observed, 'can speedily apply reheat to any dormant solution.' I stood up, dizzy with relief. 'Forget the ironing, for Pete's sake. Come and relax.'

'I'll just finish this.'

When I came back with the coffee pot she was dreamily draping the blouse on a hanger. She answered my smile with one that was not entirely free from wanness. Switching on a hotplate, I said tentatively, 'There's no one been getting at you, Val, from Kaltmans or the Security Service or wherever?'

'Of course not.' She hooked the hanger on a cupboard door. 'Whatever gave you that idea?'

CHAPTER 9

The bedside lamp went out with a pop, leaving me in semi-darkness.

After a moment's paralysis I forced myself from the bed, groped across the room and found the main switch. In the fuller light from the ceiling I stood sweating, looking around.

The curtain rippled in the breeze from the open window. Everything else lay as still as death. I went back to examine the lamp. The bulb, searing to the touch, was faintly blackened. I shoved the whole thing to the back of the bedside stand.

The breeze was chill. Shivering, I returned to bed, humping the pillow so that my head was partly raised.

Since that traumatic dinner-party, matters between

Valerie and myself had returned to an even keel. So far as I could perceive, she had forgotten the incident entirely. The Defence Ministry project had been topped and tailed, my team had dispersed, and I had begun work on a process for blast-furnace application; while Sally at her own request had been seconded to Douglas Clark to help develop a new flange design for ultra-high-speed locomotives. Any passing unpleasantness was a remote memory. Or had been until now.

Surely Valerie had forgotten?

My mind ranged in zigzag patterns, repeatedly covering the same ground, now and then identifying a new footprint. The conversation, for example, with a voice at the Town Hall.

'We did make some inquiries, Mr Tiverton. As near as we can tell, none of our rating inspectors had occasion to visit your property that day.'

'They may have had no occasion, but did anybody?'

'Not to the best of our knowledge.'

'Then there's someone going around posing as one of your people.'

'Dear me.'

'Shouldn't you notify the police?'

'We might get them to issue a warning. We do ask householders, before they let anyone into the house, to insist on seeing some proof of authority . . .'

'What proof do your chaps carry?'

He was vague about that. I asked him to find out and call me back. He never did.

Another dialogue: this time with Mel Simpson. He was being subtler than usual.

'I did say,' I reminded him, 'that as far as I was concerned, Backlash was a one-off concession to expediency. I'm not taking on another Service contract.'

'I'm not asking you to.' He gave me his bright-eyed look. 'We're better placed now, got one or two things starting to roll: the pressure's off. That's why I'm intimating – just intimating, mind – that you might feel disposed to agree to a somewhat unusual period of secondment . . .'

'I might, if I knew what it was all about.'

'Can't tell you right now, John. Good reasons. This is purely a sighting exercise. I was requested to sound you on the matter; which is what I'm doing.'

'Sight or sound,' I said irritably, 'it comes to the same thing. I'm happy with my existing programme: I know what it's scheduled for: I approve the aim. I've no desire to be shifted.'

He shrugged expressively. 'It's for you to say.'

After that he was friendlier than ever, as though anxious to demonstrate that nobody bore any hard feelings.

I tried to recall some more. But the zigzag pattern had expired at the edge of a pit; further pursuit led to nothing but a fall into a void. By skirting the pit I was able to arrive at yesterday, the afternoon spent in the library reading-room, my arrival home to walls of blankness. The period between these two episodes was an empty space. I had no mental picture to support any thesis whatever. My recollection was of two stages: standing on the footway outside the library, and then pushing open my own front door.

This could, of course, be explained. I had been deep in thought about my researches, travelling home under auto-pilotage, as a car-driver will suddenly snap out of meditation to find that he has covered a mile without conscious control. Less explicable was the apparently broader chasm that yawned earlier.

Loss of memory? It explained nothing. If I had

vanished for six months, stricken by amnesia, it seemed hardly tenable that I should return unrecognizable. Besides, the children had seemed no older. Not that I had seen Michael, but I had heard him; while Barbara I had held at arm's length, looked full in the face. 'Hallo, Daddy . . .'

A groan reached my ears.

I sat up, staring at the door. The bolt was safely in place. The nightmare feeling assailed me that I was locked in with someone who had entered while I roamed the stairs. Facing me were closet doors built into an alcove beneath the slope of the ceiling; the leading edge of one was slightly out of line with the other. I fancied a movement.

Freeing myself stealthily from the bedclothes, I looked about for something to grasp. There was nothing except the lampstand, which was held by a short flex. The groan recurred. Undoubtedly there was a quivering of the closet doors.

The window shook abruptly, rattling the fastener with a clamour that had me clutching for breath like a schoolgirl. The same gust moved the doors a little more, fetching another groan from corroded hinges.

Forcing myself away from the bed, I staggered across to wrench the doors right back, exposing three empty coat-hangers dangling from a rail inside. They clinked together as with an assumption of casualness I put my head inside to confirm to myself that there was nothing else. Breathing faster, I reclosed the doors firmly and used one of my socks to tie one knob to its twin. Then I went to the window and pulled it on to a different section of the stay.

London's lights glowed like a neon Pacific. The city lay soundless. My watch said three-twenty. The shock-proof watch with the tuning-fork action, given to me by Valerie three birthdays ago. Switching off the light, I returned to bed to wait for the sunrise.

At six-thirty the street was busier with vehicles than with people. The morning was grey and moist, like its predecessor. Dampness pursued me into the cluttered newsagent's on the corner where I had been standing for half an hour, waiting for it to open. I bought five morning papers: three populars and a couple of heavies. The shopkeeper was female and huge. 'Ta, love,' she said, giving change. 'Going to have a good old read, are we?'

Clear of the shopfront, I stopped beside some railings to scan the headlines. *Death Horror in House*. My heart and stomach lurched; but it was a report of a home accident in Cheshire. There was nothing else, front or inside pages. The *Mirror* had a paragraph about a knifing in Soho; it had happened at one a.m. *The Times* was mostly a supplement on West Africa. I went through all five of them, twice. When I was certain, I refolded the bundle and returned to the hotel.

Daylight showed it up for what it was, merely a narrow house in a terrace that had seen plusher days. Using the front-door key given to me by Mrs Carpenter, I let myself back inside, treading cautiously on the stairs to avoid disturbance: nobody was yet astir. Claiming the third-floor bathroom, I ran a warm bath and undressed, staring at my reflection in the steam-streaked mirror screwed to the wall above the washbasin.

The face was familiar enough. It looked tense; the mouth was clamped; but it was not a face that I failed to recognize. The teeth, as I bared them, delivered no shock of the unexpected: they were my teeth. The hair was tawny and thick, disordered by a sleepless night but pursuing hackneyed tracks over ears and neck. I was examining my eyes in close-up when the glass hazed over completely from the steam. The occurrence seemed symbolic. Not bothering to wipe it clear, I stepped into the bath.

Lulled by the engulfing heat into temporary euphoria, I lay back, trying to think of nothing except the certainty that in a few hours' time all would be well again; I should be parallel once more with normality. But as my body temperature adjusted, the mood slipped. The water about me became a cage. In sudden panic I heaved myself out, towelled down, got back feverishly into my clothes and escaped from the bathroom to my attic room, where I spread the newspapers over the unmade bed and studied them a third time. At eight-twenty I stuffed four of them into the waste bin, taking the *Telegraph* with me downstairs to the ground-floor passage.

Following a sign which said 'Dining-Room – Mind Your Head', I descended some further stairs leading directly into a semi-basement, a pine-clad square room containing five assorted tables laid for breakfast. As I stood irresolute, Mrs Carpenter emerged beaming from an adjoining kitchen.

'Would you like to sit there, Mr Thomas?' She indicated a long table by the window, which was about six feet below pavement level and looked out upon a vista of concrete and stone steps. The table was laid for seven. Seating myself at one end with my back to the panes, I did my best to match her cheerfulness.

'You've a good memory,' I remarked, looking for a menu.

'For names?' She laughed. 'I get lots of practice. Orange juice or cornflakes?'

'Juice, thank you.' I spoke automatically, before

becoming aware of a sensation of extreme weakness; I couldn't recall when I had last eaten. 'Sorry – could you make that cereal after all?'

'Certainly. Feeling peckish after your accident?'

I found myself staring at her. Then, remembering, I forced something approximating to a smile. 'It does seem to have had that effect.'

'You should go for a check-up.' She was speaking from the kitchen, out of view. 'Staying long in London?'

I shook open the *Telegraph*. 'It depends.'

She reappeared. 'I just wondered whether you'd be wanting the room again tonight.'

'I should hope – ' I caught myself. 'I'm planning to be elsewhere by then.'

'Oh, I see.'

She spoke good-naturedly, but I sensed an air of rebuff. To soften my words I added, 'On the offchance that I did want to come back, is it likely to be vacant again?'

She placed a hillock of cornflakes before me. 'Sure to be. I've several people leaving today, and no bookings She inspected my cutlery. 'You'll have a full breakfast? Sausage, bacon, egg and tomato.'

'You wouldn't have such a thing as a kipper?'

'Yes, I can do you a kipper, by all means. And you'd like tea or coffee? Tea.' On her way back to the kitchen she paused and turned, surveying me with a disquieting blend of concern and faint amusement. She was a small, slender person with very dark hair matched by her eyes; she looked about forty, although I guessed her looks flattered her by five years or so. 'You look a bit peaky, in my opinion,' she declared. 'Oughtn't you take things easy for a while?'

'Matters to sort out, I'm afraid.' I sprinkled a few

droplets of milk, all that there was room for, over the cornflakes, and added sugar in a spasm of voraciousness. Mrs Carpenter withdrew discreetly as feet began to clump on the stairs.

Between mouthfuls I stayed immersed in the *Telegraph*, eyeing the arriving guests in quick snatches over the sheet. Most of them were middle-aged couples, and sounded Canadian; to judge from their relationship with their hostess, they were established visitors, methodically taking in the sights of the capital and returning triumphantly each night to swop experiences at daybreak. Distributing themselves about the tables, they kept up a verbal barter while Mrs Carpenter came and went lightly with plates of food. Once or twice she caught my eye and gave me a tiny conspiratorial grin. For an insane moment I contemplated joining her in the kitchen, slamming the door on the breakfasters and confiding in her, asking her advice. Before I could yield to the impulse it occurred to me that there must be someone else out there – a male Carpenter, possibly – helping with the frying: someone to whom such an intrusion would have seemed questionable in the extreme. If there was something I wished to avoid, it was calling attention to myself. Eating my kipper as unobtrusively as possible, I chased it with two half-slices of toast and then, under cover of a barrage of cross-talk about pedestrian subways at Hyde Park Corner, slid out of my chair and made for the staircase. Mrs Carpenter spotted me leaving.

'Might see you again tonight then, Mr Thomas? I'll leave the pyjamas on the bed, just in case.'

CHAPTER 10

About thirty yards short of the house I halted to take stock.

The appearance of the street told me nothing: it lay in its habitual coma, swaddled in the moistness of the morning, its bedded cars snoring at the verges. There was no sign of human life until the sudden emergence from a gateway far ahead of a woman hauling a shopping basket on wheels which she proceeded to pack into the rear of an estate car; she then drove off. When the engine note had expired beyond the bend I covered the remaining distance to our wrought-iron gate between the laurel hedges, opened it by flicking up the metal catch, and walked along the cement path to the porch.

Lifting my hand to the bell-push, I hesitated before lowering it again to stand there with a thudding heart, telling myself it was preposterous. Preposterous that I should teeter on my own doorstep, incapable of ringing at my own front door. I glanced round. Nobody was creeping up on me. With a jerky movement I thumbed the button, heard the muted chiming inside the hall, listened for the vibrancy that would herald Valerie's quick footsteps from the rear of the house.

I had only to look at her. She couldn't keep it up, not all the time, not after the previous evening's events. For a few seconds I experienced total confidence that it was going to be all right.

The feeling endured for as long as it took me to realize that the doorbell was going unanswered. For some reason I had not been prepared for this. My plan had been

geared to commence at the moment we were face to face:
deferment of the moment threw me off balance. Again I
looked round, convinced of a trap of some kind. But the
front garden was empty, the street deserted. Giant shrubs
and a fence concealed the Elkinses' house next door. No
sound came from anywhere.

Quitting the porch, I trod across spongy grass to the
front bay window and peered through, shielding my eyes
to eliminate the reflection. The room where Elkins had
guarded me was tidy and void. The door leading into
the hall stood partly open. There was no glimpse of
movement.

Doubling back, I hurried along the side of the house
to the kitchen door. It was bolted still. A sugar bowl and
an empty glass milk jug stood on the working surface,
flush with the wall: otherwise the kitchen was clear except
for Michael's reserve tricycle, stowed under the table.

The french door at the rear was likewise secured.
Peering through, I saw that the living-room too had been
left in scrupulous order, armchairs facing each other in
solemn symmetry, magazines heaped squarely on the
coffee table. The plug of the television set had been dis-
connected from its socket. The door to the hall was shut.

My instinct was to smash a way inside. But for the
past few hours instinct had served me poorly. Instead I
stayed where I was for a while, and pondered.

The outsize spectacles worn by Miss Cardelaine gave her a
look of surprised severity, like a Disney owl. Through
them she gazed up at me from a foot-wide gap created by
the partial removal of her front door from its frame and
its retention at a point where it was poised for instantane-
ous reinstatement if a sudden need should arise. 'Yes?'
she demanded.

I said, 'Hullo, Miss Cardelaine.'

'Good morning.'

Her countenance and voice were entirely neutral. She displayed neither recognition nor alarm: simply austere appraisal. I said uselessly, 'You know who I am, don't you?'

Her mouth snapped shut, reopened. 'Perhaps I should, but I'm afraid I don't.' The door began to move towards me. 'If you're anything to do with that lunatic who – '

I spoke swiftly. 'That's what I'm here about, Miss Cardelaine. Just a few inquiries about what occurred last night.' The door travelled on. 'I'm Sergeant Thomas,' I said loudly, 'from the local CID.'

The door receded. 'You'd think I answered enough questions at the time.' Her tone was avid. 'Have you managed to catch him?'

'No . . . he's not been detained. What can you tell me about the incident, Miss Cardelaine? It could help us a great deal.'

'I can't tell you any more than what I heard.' She rested an elbow against the doorframe, pulling her spectacles down her nose as though they got in the way of concentration. 'First of all he marches in on Mrs Tiverton announcing he's her husband . . . who happens to be dead, poor soul. Won't take no for an answer, so she sends for Mr Elkins – that's her neighbour the other side – and they get rid of him. Then a bit later he turns up again, climbs into the house through an upstairs window, scares the life out of the little girl and finishes up going for Mr Elkins and knocking him downstairs. Shocking business. If you ask me,' she affirmed, taking her spectacles right off and wiping them on her apron, 'Mr Elkins was lucky not to be badly hurt.'

'He was indeed,' I agreed. 'He's back at work this

morning, I take it?'

'Oh yes. He was only out for a minute or so. The moment he was on his feet again, he insisted on helping Mrs Tiverton to pack and then ran them all to the station. Ever so good, he was. He even – '

'Mrs Tiverton's gone away, then?'

'Just for a while. Well, wouldn't you? I mean, she didn't know when this maniac might be back again, and she'd the kids to think of. Mr Elkins and I, we both advised her to go.'

'What about the house?'

'All locked up. We promised to keep an eye on it for her.'

'So if you see anyone prowling about,' I said absently, 'you'll let us know?'

'Oh, you can rely on me. She's much better off staying away from home for a week or two, not a doubt of that.'

'We ought to be able to get in touch with her. Can you give me her address?'

Miss Cardelaine resumed her spectacles to give me a hard look. 'Mr Elkins might tell you.'

'How about Mrs Elkins?'

'She's away too, at the moment. Some catering course. You can get Mr Elkins this evening when he comes home.'

'Fine. Thank you.' I made departing movements, then turned back. 'I suppose you didn't catch a glimpse yourself of the man who turned up last night?'

She shook a regretful head. 'As I say, there was this rumpus and then one of your constables called to ask me some questions about Mr Tiverton. I never knew what was going on. Then later there was this other commotion – '

'Confusing for you.' I threw her a final glance; she returned it with the look of a solid citizen, always ready to help authority. 'Confusing for everybody.'

I wandered back in the direction of our house. It seemed perfectly natural to think of it as 'our house' and inevitable that I should keep gravitating towards it, as though its brickwork would suddenly throw out a sensible answer. Before reaching it, however, I stopped at another gateway.

The Leighs were our closest friends in the street. They had been the first to offer a hand when we moved in; Barbara Leigh, who was a state registered nurse, had baby-sat for us on numerous occasions. Releasing the gate, I walked slowly along yet another cement path to yet another front door and leaned on the bell-push with a mingling of hope and dread. In a way I wanted her to be out. But no sooner had I rung than I heard the rattle of an interior door and footfalls announcing a purposeful advance. I took two deep breaths, arranging my face.

The door swung fully back. No half-measures with Barbara. She peeped out with a half-smile – an instant contradiction – and waited for me to speak. As I stood gazing at her, the smile became a full one.

'Can I do something for you?'

I managed a few words. 'I was just . . . making some inquiries . . .'

There I stuck. She said helpfully, 'Is it a survey of some kind?'

The power of speech abandoned me. I stood limp, looking past her at the rather untidy hall and its ramshackle paintwork. The helpfulness of her posture graduated to uneasiness. 'I've no opinions, you know,' she said brightly, 'about anything. If you like I'll fetch my husband, he generally has more to say . . .' She glanced across a shoulder as though looking for him: I knew he was not in the house. The trite pretence seemed unworthy of her.

I stood in a sort of acrid misery, trying to map out some moves, unable to progress beyond a dull dumb confrontation that threatened to cast roots. 'What exactly,' she tried again, 'are you questioning people about? If it's washing powder for a commercial, I think every brand is magnificent. Indiscriminate, that's what I am.'

She stood awaiting a reaction that I couldn't produce. Presently she added in a tone of mystification, 'Beyond that I can't help you, I'm afraid. So sorry.' She hesitated, giving me a final chance; then apologetically closed the door in my face.

When I took notice again, I was in the centre of a shopping area to which I had evidently walked. A sign above a cleaner's told me I was in Golders Green. My calf muscles ached. Standing in the middle of a broad pavement, passed on both sides by indifferent shoppers with preoccupations of their own, I took vacant note of the surroundings and tried to formulate some method of preventing myself from going mad. Action of any kind was an answer. Everyone knew that. Fifty yards away a bus was pulling in at a stop: sprinting, I leapt aboard as it accelerated away and said to the bored West Indian conductor, 'Go to Kilburn?'

He supplied a sketchy nod. Hoisting myself to the upper deck, I occupied the rear seat to be heaved and jerked around as the driver took us over potholes and through turnings with a spurious urgency that for a time substituted for anything of a more productive nature. But before long I felt the return of an overmastering need for mental exercise that might carry me forward instead of in circles. I pulled out my wallet.

It held two pound notes and the jottings book. Nothing legible, according to Sergeant Barker. Leafing through it, I saw that he was right. The entries seemed to consist of a kind of Speedhand, unintelligible to me, albeit in a recess of my brain lurked the notion that once it had meant something: something significant.

One entry read: 'Sp ls – kprs, bl cf, sw t. Rl-nk swrs. H bs.' And beneath, on the same page: 'Sp dsl – b eggs.'

The final word meant something, but what? A shopping list? I flipped the page. 'B – 16369; M – 91172. B – fl hr, sl, bl es. M – br hr, chby, gr es, sl lp.'

It went on like this through half the book, which had lined pages between plastic covers and looked well-thumbed. The later pages were blank. For a few minutes as the bus swung into a series of corners, my brain raced; then listlessness washed back. Without the key, there was no fathoming such gibberish. Returning the book and wallet to my inside pocket, I explored the outer ones.

They yielded nothing, as when I had examined them in the hotel attic the previous night and again that morning. The clothes I was wearing were unmarked, anonymous. Trousers of a smooth tweed, slightly flared at the ankles, with hipster belt; long-sleeved pale pink shirt under a slim sweater of bottle green with a turtle neck; a dark fawn corduroy jacket fashioned like a modified egg-timer. The shoes were of brown patent leather, very comfortable, each sporting a decorative buckle. No tags, no labels. The socks were of speckled grey and orange nylon. The underpants were the brief, hip-hugging variety, in deep blue striped with crimson, like bathing trunks.

Stripping the night before, I had scrutinized minutely every item. Dressing in the morning light, I had gone over them again, hunting for a clue, a hint. Finding nothing, I had stood back to study them with a mind wiped clean, in the desperate hope that something about them might strum a chord which made listenable music. Nothing did.

An unusually emphatic lurch of the bus made me glance through the window. We had reached Kilburn. I recognized it, not as a place with which I was intimately familiar but as one that had been shown to me, perhaps many times, so that I knew it as one might know a face observed regularly across a Tube train, acquainted with its features while having to guess at the personality which lay behind. Rising, I swung myself downstairs. The conductor in a moment of revival said, 'Hutchinson's. Everybody out for a spend-up.' He flashed a white-toothed grin at a girl hunched on a nearby seat; she stared back impassively. For a fleeting instant I felt sorry for him. I jumped off.

CHAPTER 11

The motor explosion had hit Kaltmans. Traversing the concrete forecourt, I had to weave between the cars that bulged over their marking lines like plump women forced into slimline blouses. A face behind the glass frontage of the kiosk outside the building surveyed my approach. As I came level, the glazed hatch was pulled aside.

'Help you, sir?'

A lean-faced man with humorous eyes beneath a peaked cap. Theobald Parkes. The name came to me easily. Last year Theo had received a brass clock and a picnic hamper to mark his completion of thirty years with the company, replying with a speech of thanks that had been acclaimed as the funniest of the decade. A month afterwards, he and his wife had lost their only daughter when she fell on the line at Moorgate Tube Station. Within three days he had been back inside his kiosk at the main

entrance, working off the concussion. There was nobody
in the firm whom he could not have identified on a dark
night by the note of their voice. He knew of all that went
on and he kept it under his official cap with a massive
discretion that had earned him the confidence of everyone
from the boardroom to the canteen. Nothing and nobody
got past ex-Sergeant Parkes of the Royal Fusiliers. I
altered course towards him.

'Only me, Theo.'

The humour remained in evidence behind the gravity
with which he surveyed me. 'Got an appointment, have
you, sir?'

'Oh God,' I said. 'Not you as well.'

Wary puzzlement added itself to the solemnity. When
he spoke again he was very courteous. Theo never got
fussed. 'If you'll give me the name of the person you want
to see, sir, I'll phone through and – '

'Go to hell.'

Turning away, I made for the entrance steps. I had
reached the fourth when my progress was impeded. For a
man of sixty-two, Theo could move fast.

'Very sorry, sir, but I'm not allowed to permit un-
authorized entry. It'll just take – '

'For Christ's sake, man. I work here, don't I?'

The latter phrase was more question than pronounce-
ment. He seemed to detect this. Before replying he delayed
a few moments, running a careful gaze over me as though
punching lines of information on to cerebral dockets and
cross-referring. Momentarily his eyes went opaque as the
central computer tapped out an answer. Then they
cleared again; clearer than a pool in a burn.

'Think you must have made a mistake, sir,' he said
firmly. 'It *was* Kaltmans you were looking for?'

He was throwing me a lifeline. It struck me full on the

temple, detonating a blast that was pursued by a feeling of muscular atrophy which made me reach out for support. Swaying to one side, I rested on the handrail. He moved across too, keeping me within arm's length.

'Yes, it was Kaltmans all right,' I said apathetically. 'There is a Mr Simpson on the staff here?'

'You've an appointment with someone of that name?' The courtesy was unshakeable.

'Tell him I'm here, will you?'

'Your name, sir?'

I looked back at him. There was nothing in his face but the wish to know.

'John Tiverton,' I said.

He was silent for a moment.

'A relation, sir?'

'Pardon?'

'We did have a gentleman of that name with us until quite recently. I wondered if – '

'Oh yes.' I gave a sudden laugh; the amusement was real. 'I'm related all right. Couldn't be closer.'

'I see, sir. Well now, if you'll kindly come back with me to the hut over there . . .'

A new look entered his pupils. I realized I had made a movement of some kind, sinew-tensing perhaps; I was on the brink of breaking past him, smashing a way into the building, bursting in on people; at the tail-end of the very last second I hauled myself back. That wasn't the way. If I involved myself again with the police I was finished: my freedom of action would be gone. To get round a conspiracy, something subtler was needed. I returned with him meekly to the kiosk.

It was characteristic of Theo that he had the honesty to call it a hut. I had the feeling that if a conspiracy existed, he wasn't part of it. And yet, how could he not be? Perhaps it was merely that I craved to have that feeling. Inviting me with a gesture to stand at the hatch, he went inside, lifted the phone and said conversationally after a second or two, 'Research section, Vera, would you mind?' Covering the mouthpiece, he said through the hatch: 'Brother of Mr Tiverton's, sir?'

'Cousin.'

'I see . . . That you, Mrs Garfield? Theobald. I've a gentleman here to see Mr Simpson: understand he's a cousin of – Oh, is he? But he's not been past me here. Ah, I follow. Hang on a minute.' He held the phone away. 'Mr Simpson's away, sir, just now. Won't be back today, I'm afraid.'

'Miss Masters, then.'

His eyebrows bunched slightly. 'You mean Mrs Clark?'

'I mean Sally Masters.'

'Yes: Mrs Clark, she is now. Married a couple of months back. She doesn't work here any more.'

I took a few breaths, as rhythmically as possible.

'Anyone in research, then.'

Theo was keeping his head. He said smoothly into the receiver, 'Gentleman would like if possible to see anybody in research who's available . . . Tiverton. That's right, yes, he's a cousin. Well, nor was I, but . . .' He began to choose his words. 'No, I wouldn't think so. I can if you like. Hold on.' He turned back. 'Fairly strict security around here, sir: sure you'll understand if I ask you for any proof of identity, anything that we can . . .'

I patted pockets. 'Left my wallet at home, unfortunately. It has my driving licence inside. There's nothing else.'

He sucked in his lower lip. 'Tiny bit awkward . . .'

'It needn't be awkward,' I said, keeping my tone level, 'if you'd allow me through to the reception area. That's well apart from the labs, isn't it? I only want a

word with someone . . . Frank Selby would be fine, or
Joan Petworth – anyone like that. I wouldn't keep them
more than a few minutes, and I certainly wouldn't be a
nuisance.'

The expression of calculation had returned; he seemed
to be running a playback of my words. He reached a
decision.

'Miss Petworth able to get away?' he asked the telephone. 'Think she'd mind popping along to the foyer?
Mr Tiverton says he just wants a quick word.'

Presently he said, 'Ta, dear,' and replaced the receiver.
'Miss Petworth'll be along,' he told me kindly. 'I'll
take you across.'

I let him shepherd me to the foyer. We stood side by
side in the unwelcoming oblong, a masterpiece of instant
repellence in naked buff brickwork and heavily-scuffed
light blue acoustic floor tiling. The building was encased
in its usual bleak silence. To puncture it I said, 'So Sally
Masters is a housewife now? Clark . . . Would that be
Douglas, the locomotion specialist?'

Theo gave me one more of his searching looks. 'You
seem to know a lot about us, sir.'

'Family gossip,' I said carelessly.

His lips pursed. We said nothing more. A distant tip-
tapping became audible, swelling to become something
tangible in the formless shape of Joan, wearing a laboratory
smock and a facial mask of irritation which she composed,
too late, into one of friendly inquiry. She glanced from
me to Theo and back to me. Her eyes were entirely
blank.

'Mr Tiverton?' she asked.

'That's right.' The challenge was prominent in my
voice. We stared at one another. Her vacuity seemed as
genuine as that of all the others. She waited for me to go

on; when I didn't she became ill at ease. Obviously she
felt disinclined to exert herself to loosen a tight social
situation. Theo moved himself diplomatically into the
picture.

'Mr Tiverton's a relation of *our* Mr Tiverton, Miss
Petworth. Cousin, in fact.'

'Really? I wondered when I heard the name. Is there
something we can do for you, Mr Tiverton?'

Her almond-shaped grey eyes were screwed up in
synthetic goodwill. I couldn't meet them any more.
Staring past her along the corridor from which she had
come, I said, 'Yes, there was something. I'm anxious to
learn a little about . . . what happened to him. I've been
away, you see.'

She shot Theo a look. 'His widow is still living in their
old home, I believe. . .'

'We don't hit it off too well,' I explained. 'I didn't
want to intrude on her if it could be helped.'

'No, I see.' She pushed fingers through her wild mousy
hair. 'I'm not sure there's all that much I can tell you.
It was a motor accident, you knew that? Back in the late
spring. Your . . . your cousin was driving home from a
weekend conference at Eastbourne when his car went out
of control on a curvy road and piled into a ditch. He wasn't
wearing a seat-belt and he was flung through the windscreen.' She paused. 'He didn't recover consciousness.'

'Is that quite certain?'

'What?'

'That he never came round.'

Shadows of faint shock drifted across her face. 'That's
what was stated,' she said severely, 'at the inquest.'

'When was that held?'

'The inquest? A few weeks later, I suppose. They
generally are.'

'Did it get much publicity?'

'Not that I recall.' She looked interrogatively at Theo, who shook a solemn head. 'There may have been a paragraph here and there when it first happened, but I doubt if the inquest was reported – except in the local paper, probably.'

'Where exactly did it happen?'

'The accident? Near a village in Sussex called . . .' Joan's lank tresses underwent further disarrangement. 'Herringly? Some name like that.'

Weakness had been attacking my knees for some minutes. Theo said alertly, 'Like a chair, sir, for a little while?'

'Thanks, no . . . I'm all right.' I rested a shoulder against the brickwork, my own voice reaching me as though from the far end of a tunnel. 'When you say he – my cousin didn't regain consciousness, does that mean he lingered for a time?'

'So we understood,' Joan said reluctantly.

'They wouldn't have tried plastic surgery on him?'

'Before he even recovered?' Her outrage filled the foyer.

I said defensively, 'I don't know much about these things. It just occurred to me, if his face was badly smashed they might have seized the chance while he was unconscious anyway – '

'They'd have been too busy trying to keep him alive. Besides,' said Joan, taking a quick look at the electric clock on the opposite wall, 'you can't perform plastic surgery on someone till the wounds have healed and they're in a state to take it. It's just not on.'

She was getting restive. The clock showed that it was coming up to noon; she liked to take an early lunch, I remembered, and woe betide anyone who interfered with her fancies.

'I won't trouble you any longer,' I said. 'Very grateful, Joan.'

If she was startled at the familiarity she gave no sign. 'Shouldn't think I've been much help,' she observed on a note of relief, 'but then we never heard details of the accident. If you like I can give you his widow's address – '

'I have it, thanks. As I say, I'm not keen to inflict myself on her. Thanks again for talking to me.'

She shook my hand with the enthusiasm of release. 'Very welcome. We were so sorry about your cousin. Bye bye.' Pivoting on platform soles, she hurried off, not glancing back.

Theo stepped into my sightline. I couldn't tell how long I had stood there, staring after Joan. His voice held a cautionary ring. 'Nobody else you want to see, Mr Tiverton?'

'Not here.' I swallowed, fighting off dizziness. 'Not today, at least. I might . . . might try to contact Mr Simpson later. But I would like to see Miss Masters – Mrs Clark, that is. Would you be able to let me have her home address, by any chance?'

'No, sir,' he said promptly. 'That's something I'm not at liberty to reveal.'

'Then can I ask one more favour?'

'Never a bit of harm in asking,' he admitted with a glimpse of the humour.

'Could you telephone Mrs Clark for me, explain who I am and ask if she'd mind my calling on her?'

He thought about it. 'Don't see a lot of harm in that, neither. Follow us back to the hut, sir?'

As he held the swing door for me, I hesitated. Something like a smothered laugh had reached my ears. Experimentally I moved a shoe across the floor tiling: it produced a sound that was not dissimilar, but a doubt remained. Theo was eyeing me oddly. My gaze swept the foyer, meeting nothing but the bald walls and the hyper-modernistic furniture. I stepped outside.

'Bizarre place to work in,' I commented as we descended the steps.

There was sudden extra warmth to his smile. 'Just what your cousin used to say, sir.'

CHAPTER 12

The flats were a superior example of the high-rise variety close to the summit of Highgate. From the upper floors the outlook must have been spectacular. The Clarks were second-floor occupants, which surprised me; it seemed to run counter to Doug Clark's penthouse personality. Marriage, however, changed things . . . and people. It was common knowledge. Mounting the cork-lined stairway, I reminded myself how surprised I was that the Clarks should dwell on the second floor instead of the fourteenth.

The reminder was necessary because, for the moment, actual surprise was outside the compass of my capabilities. There was no space for it among the reactions I was left with. To reason out what I ought to be feeling at given points was a mind-rescuing substitute, helping to keep me just this side of sanity.

There were no corridors in the block. It had been laid out craftily, all rectangular areas and doors facing different ways. This made number twelve hard to find until I came upon it accidentally behind an arched opening. While I was ringing I had time to notice that there was, in fact, a tremendous view right across London from this

flank of the building; which made me think that Doug
Clark had known after all what he was up to, as had
seemed probable from the start. Inside the flat there were
multifarious sounds. Above all I could hear the thunder-
ings of a symphony orchestra in rich stereophonic ampli-
fication: the work being played was strange to me.
Absorbed in its themes, I delayed my second ring. I was
lifting a hand to administer it when the door opened.

'Had you buzzed?' Sally asked above the music. 'I
caught sight of your outline through the glass, actually.
Otherwise I'd never have known. Wait a second . . .'

Darting back across the square hallway, she reduced
the volume almost to nothing. Then returned, smiling.
She was clad with careless elegance in a tunic blouse and
bright red satin trousers; her platinum hair was dragged
back and tied behind in a coil. She rested a hand grace-
fully upon a hip. 'Theo rang me from Kaltmans before
lunch and said you'd be along shortly after two, so I was
keeping a lookout. Do come in. Forgive the shambles.'

When I made no movement her smile faded a little.
'I've not dropped a frightful clanger?' she demanded.
'You're not from North Sea Gas or something?'

All I could do was gape at her. An element of impatience
intruded on her vivacity.

'Please *say* something. You have come from Kaltmans?
You are John's cousin?'

My voice was a croak. 'That's it – Kaltmans. I was
hoping you might recognize me, Sally.'

She looked taken aback. 'We never met, did we?
I'm sorry . . . if we did I've forgotten. Shocking memory for
faces. Of course I knew John very well. Were you close
cousins? Can't spot a family resemblance, I must say.
Look, do come in.'

I shuffled into the centre of the hallway. Closing the

door, she walked past me into the large, brightly decorated square living-room in which a faint vibrancy was now the sole indicator of stereophonic activity. She stooped over the turntable and the vibrations ceased. 'I play it too loud, they tell me,' she remarked, turning back to me. 'But it seems a waste of all that apparatus otherwise. Come through. Have a chair. Like a cup of tea? Coffee?'

I sank into a corner of the settee, spacious and square like the accommodation. From there I gazed up at her. My wordless scrutiny began to have an effect: giving her coil of hair a nervous poke, she forced a laugh.

'I'll say this, you're less talkative than John was. By now he'd have been well into his third wind and I'd have had bruised eardrums.' She perched opposite me on the end of a padded footrest. 'To be honest, I wasn't aware John had any cousins. I always understood he came from a smallish, close-knit family. Perhaps he didn't know himself. I dare say a lot of us are ignorant of our far-flung connections – until something happens, anyway, and the strands start coming together . . .' She was talking as though apprehensive of a silence. The fingers of her right hand kneaded the footrest padding. 'I take it you've only just heard about what happened to John? Have you been abroad somewhere?'

I said abruptly, 'I'm not his cousin.'

Her head jerked back. She made no sound: it was all movement, tiny gestures. Her right hand tightened on the padding; her left rose to her throat. I could see her holding her breath. Her eyes flickered towards the hall-way before switching back to rest on me again, radiating the brightness which showed that she was thinking hard. As I leaned forward with an elbow on a knee, she flinched.

'Don't be alarmed,' I went on. 'I haven't bluffed my way in to do you any harm. It's just that something strange is going on. I want your help.'

'Something strange?' She spoke on the surface of a gasp.

'Yes. The strangest thing, almost, is that you're sitting there calling me John Tiverton's cousin. I'm not, you know.'

'Who are you, then?'

'I'm John Tiverton himself.'

After an interval of staring she released a small shaky laugh. 'You mean your name's John Tiverton as well? But you're no relation?'

'I'm John Tiverton,' I insisted. 'The one you know at Kaltmans. Knew, rather. Think, Sally. You recognize me now, don't you?'

Expressions were chasing each other across her features. None of them was the one I wanted to see, the lighting up of widened eyes, the dawning intelligence. Only bemusement, dismay, the seeds of fear. I itched to leap across the intervening space, to shake her by the shoulders, roar at her. Holding myself on a tight rein, I spoke calmly, reasonably.

'As I mentioned, something very odd is taking place. I can see you don't know me. Just like all the rest. Nevertheless there's no getting away from it: I'm the guy you were working with on Project Backlash a few months ago; the one you came to dinner with a couple of times, him and his wife Valerie; the one who . . . Remember Carmino's? The Spanish joint near Paddington where we used to eat, you and me? Seeing Joan reminded me. Joan Petworth at the lab, our fork-tongued spinster with the flashes of genius. She didn't know me either, but I could tell you everything about her that you know yourself . . . for the very good reason that it was you who told me. Frank Selby, who brought you to our place that time. Not to mention the sphinx-like Phillison . . .'

Her eyes were in a frown of sheer concentration: she was absorbing every syllable. Her lips were slightly parted. The fright was being gradually replaced by an apparent anger, which broke out from her as I paused for breath.

'What utter rubbish! Just what are you playing at? I knew John Tiverton – of course I did. You're not him. Nothing like him. How dare you walk in here and maintain that you are?'

'Just like all the rest,' I repeated miserably.

'You mean you've been to the others with this story?' Rising from the footrest, she reseated herself on a chair-back a little farther away and surveyed me across folded arms. 'Are you quite mad?'

'I'm not mad,' I said quietly. 'What I'm starting to ask myself is whether everyone else is.'

'Usually an infallible sign.' She smouldered for a moment. 'What reaction did you get at Kaltmans, may I ask?'

'The same. And Valerie didn't know me either.'

'That doesn't stagger me in the least. She's been a widow for half a year.'

'How do you know?'

Sally stared. 'Because her husband was killed, that's how.'

'Did you see his body?'

'Oh, for God's sake.' She got up, walked into the hall-way, returned to stand gripping the chair-back with both hands. 'One doesn't normally query these things. Besides it's irrelevant. I don't have to ask myself whether you might conceivably be John: I know you're not.'

'Suppose my face had been reshaped.' I paused. 'Surgically. Would the rest of me fit?'

It pulled her up. She examined me with a new look in her eyes, one of reluctant surmise and assessment. Finally she shook a decisive head. 'The height and build might just pass,' she said with the same smoking anger, 'but for a face to be transformed so radically in such a space of time – it's not feasible . . .'

'Take a closer look.'

Remaining seated, I brought my body forward, up-turning my face. Hesitantly she moved over to peer into it from a yard's range. 'No sign of tampering,' she announced, retreating again. 'It's impossible.'

'Don't be hasty.'

'John had a lean face with high cheekbones. Yours is broader – much broader. Your eyes are set wider apart and the nose is different altogether. It couldn't be done.'

She was back in her former stance, glowering at me. At least she had made no move towards the telephone. I sat back.

'Okay. We rule out plastic surgery. How about this? The first time you came to dinner with Val and me we had grilled sole and iced gâteau. You and she got on well. You laughed together about Government training colleges. Later you had a cup and a half of coffee and spilt some on the rug. You left a bar of chocolate for the kids. Cadbury's Dairy Milk.'

I kept my gaze on her. 'The second time was a near-disaster. You and I were the only ones who talked. Frank Selby sulked and Phillison kept to himself and Val went silent. Next day in the lab we had a few words about it. But we still worked together on Backlash. Once you remarked that you'd be glad when it was over because it made you feel like one of the dogs of war, and I said that according to Mel Simpson the real war was on the economic front and therefore we were all part of the pack; to which you replied that some of its elements tended to be bitchier than others . . .'

By now Sally's face was expressionless. I wondered whether she was listening, but I ploughed on. 'One evening you got me to keep you late, working on some graphs, so that you wouldn't have to go to a concert with Frank. That was the time I said as we left: "Two more days and we can wrap this up." And you said: "As far as I'm concerned that's two days more than I can stand." And as you said it, you tripped over a lifted floor-tile and went flat on your face. While I was picking you up – '

'Any of this,' she interrupted, 'you could have got from other people.'

'All this detail?'

'I've a tendency to sound off to my friends. I give them chapter and verse.'

'But why the hell should I go around making inquiries about it?'

'You tell me. You're the one comes bursting in here with some fairytale about being John Tiverton . . . what motive you could possibly have I don't begin to understand, but I do accept the evidence of my own senses. I happen to be a scientist. I deal in realities.'

'I thought I did,' I said bitterly.

'Well, go away and start trying. If you came here hoping to get something out of me, you can regard the attempt as a failure. My advice to you, whoever you are, is to stop playing with fire. It could leave you with some first-degree burns.' She stood looking down at me. 'Now if you don't mind I'll see you out.'

I came slowly to my feet. 'Happy with Doug, are you, Solio?'

Her intake of breath was only partially concealed.

I saw her hands clench. 'Did you think I'd forget?' I inquired. 'It was a good nickname. Suited you. Things like that don't pass out of one's mind.'

She recovered speedily. 'Especially when one's only just learned them.'

I shook my head. 'It was special to us. I used it on rare occasions – remember?'

'I probably blabbed it to someone. Joan.'

'You were never on that sort of confidential basis with her.'

'A lot you know about women.' She seemed to be talking to gain time; her gaze was once more dusting me down. 'Anyway, if it answers your question I'm perfectly happy with Doug, thanks. We get along fine, and it's no business of yours.'

'Fast-tempered as ever, is he? Liable to snap?' I feigned meditation. 'As I recall, it was supposed to be all due to his upbringing: that horrendous childhood with an over-indulgent mum. Though your view was that it was his Celtic blood. And when all's said and done, nobody can help being born in a place like Llanberis . . .'

I studied the effect on her. She was doing her best, but the effort was starting to show. She shook her head with an almost masochistic violence.

'You could still have picked all this up. Anyone could.'

'Tell me why.'

'No – you explain to me.'

'Can't you see?' I implored. 'There's no explanation. It's beyond comprehension. I'm John Tiverton, he exists in my skin – surely I've said enough to convince you of that? And yet nobody acknowledges me. My wife, my own mother – '

I stopped. She said unsteadily, 'If your own mother doesn't know you, how could anybody?'

'She hasn't seen me,' I said with a mounting excitement.
'Then how – '
'I spoke to her, that's all. On the phone. She lives in Newcastle.'
'Well, what did she say?'
'Told me to get off the line. Said I'd been dead for six months.'
'There you are, you see. The accident – '
I seized her arms. 'That's exactly it. She thinks what all of you think: that I was killed in a car crash. She doesn't question it. So naturally she took me for an impostor.'
'Of course she doesn't question it. She probably identified the – the body.'
'She might not have done. Could have been Val.'
'So why doesn't *she* question it?'
'She could be in it.'
'In what?'
'Whatever's going on.'
'If she is, then we all are.' Sally had made no attempt to release herself from my grasp. She was watching me with a close intensity, apparently prepared to meet me halfway, to thrash the thing through. 'Look here, though – how about your voice? Didn't Valerie recognize that?'
'Do you?'
She frowned. 'It's not unlike John's. But then he had a very neutral sort of delivery. Standard English, same as yours.'
'But the intonation, the timbre?'
She shrugged. 'Similar. That's as far as I'd go.'
'If I was in a smash, it could have altered my voice.'
'You're obsessed about this accident. Sure you've not been in one yourself and got confused?'
'Would it knock me into a dead man's shoes? I just don't believe in that sort of trauma. If I'm obsessed about

the crash, it's because I don't believe it ever occurred . . .
or not as it's supposed to have done. I'll be checking on
that.' I considered for a few moments. 'In the meantime,
Sally, I want you to do a small thing for me. A tiny
thing. I want you to agree with me that there's a possibility – just that, a possibility – that I could be who I say
I am. I ask no more. Simply to give me a foot touching
the ground. Will you do that?'

She pulled away and I let her go. Walking through
the hallway to the outer door of the flat, she opened it
and stepped outside. From there she looked back.

'I'm going to scream for help.'

I transmitted a gesture. 'Okay,' I said wearily. 'I
can't stop you. Let's get it over.'

Returning inside, she closed the door and slipped the
catch. She faced me again with brilliance in her violet
eyes.

'There's a way,' she said softly, 'that I could really
tell whether you might be John Tiverton. Want to put
it to the test?'

CHAPTER 13

'Well?' I asked.

She stirred beneath the eiderdown. Her voice was husky.
'I don't know, darling. I just don't know.'

The savagery of my disappointment brought me up on
to an elbow. Seizing her by the chin, I turned her face
towards mine. 'You can't get away with that,' I shouted.
'You can't just . . . use me and then leave me in mid-air.'

'I can't do anything else,' she protested. 'Ouch, you're
hurting. It was an idea that didn't come off, that's all

there is about it.'

I lay fuming. 'You knew things were never really like that with us.'

'Weren't they?' She spoke demurely. 'Not with John?'

'All right. You and I may have had one or two good times together. That's all they were. It was over long since.'

'I never said it wasn't,' she murmured.

'So we agree? So how would I have known a thing like that?'

'Could have been a lucky guess.'

She smiled up at me past a soft white shoulder. I threw myself back to lie staring at the ceiling.

'I'm not sure where it's got us,' I muttered.

She turned towards me. 'Neither am I,' she said, businesslike. 'I'll tell you this, quite frankly: I enjoyed it. But then I do enjoy it. If you were John, you'd know that. And if you weren't John but had made the inquiries you seem to have done, you'd have found it out. I've no illusions about my reputation.'

'But it hasn't got *me* anywhere.'

'I'm sorry.'

I consulted my watch. 'What time does Doug . . .?'

'You should know what time he leaves the lab.'

'Five, it used to be.' I glanced at her; she nodded. 'How long does it take him to get here?'

'He'll be home about half past.'

'It's turned four.' I got off the bed. 'I'd better make myself scarce.'

While I dressed she lay with hands behind her head, contemplating my movements with an unabashed interest. Presently she said, 'This car crash. There'd have been an official report on it at the time, surely?'

'Police report? Presumably.'

'Why not ask about it?'

'Don't worry.' I glanced up from my sock-straightening. 'How did you first come to hear about it?'

'The crash? At the lab.'

'Who from?'

'Frank Selby or someone,' she said vaguely. 'The word went buzzing around . . . you know how it is.'

'Yes, I do know. But I thought I wasn't supposed to?'

'I'm keeping an open mind. I want to help if possible. After all, I have to admit I never actually saw John's body, or even went to the funeral, for that matter. Cremation was private. At least, that's what . . .' Her voice tailed off. I glanced up again. 'I remember now,' she went on. 'It was Mel Simpson who first came in full of it. Terribly upset, he was. Really shattered – you'd have been moved if you could have seen him. Is that what I mean to say? Gets complicated.'

'Did he say I was dead? Try to remember his exact words.'

Freeing her right arm, she placed it across her forehead. 'If I'm not mistaken, he said you were critical. Said John was critical.'

'And then later . . .?'

'A few days after that we heard the worst.'

'Again from Mel?'

'Yes, I believe so. In the first instance.'

'Wasn't there anything in the papers?'

'Mm. An inquest report in the local sheet. It said . . . let's see . . . said the road surface and camber at the spot were notoriously treacherous and it was raining at the time.'

'Verdict?'

'Accidental – what else? There was some jury recommendation about having the road seen to.'

Pulling on my sweater, I smoothed my hair and grabbed my jacket.

'Tell us one other thing, Sally. Having completed Backlash, did we then go back to civilian projects . . . or take on another military contract?'

'Can't tell you that,' she said.

'Oh, come on. It's vital.'

'If you were who you say you are,' she said with emphasis, 'you'd know I can't tell you.'

I stood staring at the floor.

'Enjoy being at home?' I asked.

'What?'

'Doesn't seem like you – the housewife bit.'

'Oh that. I'd have stayed on at Kaltmans, only Doug's a shade possessive. Said he didn't fancy me being available to all and sundry at the lab once we were wed. So, to oblige, I quit.'

'You don't get bored?'

'Nope.' She smiled disarmingly. 'Plenty of extremely good friends in the neighbourhood.'

'I'm sure. Just the same, I'd have thought your salary would have come in useful.'

'Doug wangled himself a fat rise.'

'How'd he manage that?'

'I gather Mel spoke up for him.'

'Did he now?'

She moved restively. 'Time I was getting myself decent. Want to wait in the other room?'

'No, I'm off. Sally . . .' I hesitated. 'This sounds terrible. But I'm in a sticky position and I've just two quid on me. Unless I get this cleared up by tonight – '

'God,' she said with a hollow laugh, 'I'm having to pay 'em now. Fetch me my purse, will you? Five be enough?'

I gave her a swift kiss. 'Honestly it's not what you think. I must have cash so that I can get around and put an end to this nightmare. You'll have it back.'

'Naturally. Best of luck.'

At the doorway I turned. She was regarding me curiously from the pillow. I gave her a flip of the hand to which she responded with a small shake of the head. 'Try Tony Phillison,' she said.

The front office of the *Recorder* was stuffy and varnished. The same adjectives applied with equivalent force to the female custodian of the small ads counter, an elderly woman in a grey cardigan who, meeting my request in silence, brooded upon it for several minutes while attending to a customer who couldn't think how to word an advertisement for a lady to come in twice a week to vacuum the floors. When the problem had been resolved, she raised the counter flap and stalked to a rack near the window overlooking the street. A flick of a taloned hand brought down a bound file of newspapers out of a line of others. 'You should find what you want in there,' she affirmed, looking the opposite way as though her eyes were hurting. She returned in a sequence of pedestrian clicks to her fortress, slamming the flap back into place.

'Thank you,' I said politely.

The file covered a three-month period ending four months previously. I worked back. There seemed to have been innumerable gatherings of the District Amenities Society, Over Sixties Clubs and the Chamber of Trade. The newsprint smelt of inky dust. A local councillor called Brian Harding had attended virtually every event in the calendar, managing a contentious declaration at each: 'Harding Hits at Rates Chaos' . . . 'Street Lights Dim-out Slammed by Councillor' . . . The gentleman was free with his suggestions. They all made good headlines. The last date in the file was April 2nd. Returning to June, I went through more methodically, not forgetting the small-ads pages; and it was on one of these, in the issue dated May 21, that I spotted what I was looking for.

In a corner of the page allocated to news, a single-column item was headed 'Fatal Smash After Skid'. The report began:

'A Finchley man whose car rolled into a ditch in a Sussex lane died in hospital four days later, a Lewes inquest heard on Tuesday.

'He was Mr John Tiverton, aged 37, of The Park, who was an industrial research scientist.

'Cause of the crash was said to be heavy rain and bad visibility coupled with the state of the road surface, which . . .'

In the view of Police-Sergeant Malcolm Foster, who attended the scene, the surface became treacherous in rain and the cambers on the bends were exceptionally adverse. Two other accidents, neither of them fatal, had occurred on the same stretch within the previous two months.

Evidence as to the length of skid-marks and other traces was given by a Police-Constable William Marks. It seemed I had been thrown through the shattered windscreen, sustaining head injuries that had kept me in a coma until my death.

A pathologist, Dr E. P. Klein, had carried out a post-mortem examination but was unable to say positively whether any particular physical factor could have contributed to the loss of control. Returning a verdict of accidental death, the jury asked that some attention should be given to the lane by 'the authorities'.

I carried the file across to the counter. From the other end the custodian spoke instantly with her face averted. 'Have you finished with it?'

'Not quite.' I looked at her until she sent me a glance to find out whether I was still there. 'This news item,' I said, pointing to it. 'Would that have been written by someone here?'

With vast reluctance she crab-walked closer to examine it. Her head flapped. 'Not if it took place in Sussex, no.'

'Who, then, do you think?'

'Couldn't say.' She sniffed a couple of times. 'Do you want to see someone from Editorial?'

'Please, if that's possible.'

Sniffing again, she depressed a buzzer and went away.

A long interval was terminated by the appearance of a youth with a cadaverous face and greasy hanging hair who was directed towards me by a cranial jerk from the harridan. I showed him the report.

'Something wrong with it?' he asked touchily.

'I don't know. But I'd like to know where you got it from. Can you tell me that?'

He scanned it again with a slackened jaw. 'Lewes,' he pronounced finally. 'That would have been sent to us on linage. Agency report.'

'I see. Reliable, are they?'

'Oh, very.'

'There's no possibility that this could have been a fake story?'

He gave me a keen glare. 'What makes you think it might have been?'

'I'm just asking.'

He stood back against the counter, resting his elbows. 'But you must have some reason. Is it inaccurate?'

'As I said, I'm not sure. It could be.'

He reflected. 'I could check,' he offered, 'with the chief sub.'

'Would you do that?'

'Sure. Can I have your name?'

'Charles Thomas,' I told him.

While I was waiting, a plump youngish woman with fair, frizzy hair entered to place a small-ad. Her first perfunctory glance in my direction was followed by a second and a third, less sketchy, as she wrote out her requirements at the far end of the counter. I was certain I didn't know her. At the third inspection I began to feel irritated, and to avoid her eyes I re-read the report.

It was much like the account of any other inquest I had ever skimmed. Every word gave off an authentic ring. Every word except two: the name of the subject. Could there conceivably be another research scientist called John Tiverton of The Park, Finchley? 'Industrial research' – the term was comprehensive enough to embrace a wide cross-section. 'Head injuries' – another blanket phrase. Now that I was looking at it again, the report seemed to contain more that was questionable than I had initially thought. Why was the pathologist unable to be more definite?

Concluding her business, the fair-haired woman carried out a fourth covert inspection of me before leaving. I checked my watch with the office clock: they agreed on five-fifteen.

The youth reappeared. 'He remembers the story,' he announced without preamble. 'Came from the Lewes agency: had their stamp on it. And apart from that, one of the subs had to phone 'em to check on something.'

'So it was no fake?'

'Absolutely not. Can I ask you – '

'Many thanks,' I said swiftly. 'All I wanted to know.' Leaving the file on the counter, I left the office.

I looked both ways along the street. Fifty yards to my right, the fair-haired woman was staring into a chemist's window. I began walking rapidly, easing up as I approached her, finally halting at her elbow. I said, 'Excuse me . . .'

She jumped and swung. 'Yes?'

'Do forgive me, but I couldn't help noticing you in the newspaper office just now. I may be wrong, but . . . I got the idea you were under the impression you knew me?'

She was staring at me, the way I had been stared at so many times in the past twenty-four hours; or nearly in that way. After a moment she said confusedly, 'I'm terribly sorry – I didn't mean to be rude. You did remind me of someone, as a matter of fact.'

I kept my voice light. 'But now that you look at me closer, I don't?'

'Well . . . you are quite like him. But then I don't know this person awfully well anyway. He's more an acquaintance of my husband's.'

'If I *were* him,' I said playfully, 'would I know you?'

'Oh, I doubt it. I've only seen you – seen this person a couple of times . . . from a distance, you know. At meetings.'

'May I ask what sort of meetings?'

'Industrial seminars. My husband's in machine tools.'

'Now that,' I said calmly, 'is interesting. Perhaps I'd be familiar with his name.'

'Cotter,' she said. 'Maurice Cotter.'

Her voice reached me like an echo. There was distortion, a sense of remoteness and yet at the same time an identifiable shape to the syllables. I must have stood

there longer than I intended, repeating them to myself:
becoming conscious of her once more, I observed her
subdued agitation. Again I apologized. 'I was just trying
to think . . . We could be acquainted. If you'll excuse a
rather odd question: do you happen to know the name
of this person you think I might be?'

Her stare had become fixed. She replied, however,
without prevarication. 'Yes, I do. My husband has
mentioned it several times. It's Thomas.'

CHAPTER 14

'Charles Thomas?'

'That's right. I remember my husband pointing him
out.' She paused with increasing uncertainty. 'Or you,
was it?'

'How I wish,' I said, 'I could answer that.'

She recoiled a pace towards the shop entrance. The
danger of losing her made me take a grip on myself;
I pumped up a smile of reassurance. 'At the moment,'
I explained, 'I'm having a spot of memory bother.
Temporary amnesia or something. I seem to know the
name Charles Thomas but that's as far as I get. You
weren't told of an address, by any chance?'

'I'm afraid I know nothing whatever about Mr Thomas,
other than his name.' Obviously she was making an effort
to think with untypical speed: to decide whether she was
being appealed to for help, or conned. I leaned tiredly
against the plate-glass window of the chemist's. Her tone
softened. 'I tell you what. Perhaps my husband could help.'

'Will he be at home?'

'Not yet, but we could call into his office – it's only a

short way from here.'

'Great idea,' I said with enthusiasm. 'I'd appreciate it very much. As long as it's not putting you to a lot of trouble.'

'I was killing time anyway. It's just a few minutes' walk.' She led off downhill, back past the newspaper office in the direction of the City. 'They're in Goddard Street at the foot of the hill. Tell me about this mental block of yours – you mean you can't remember anything? Not even where you work?'

'Such recollections as I do have seem to be unreliable.' I tried to keep the sourness out of my voice. 'These seminars you were talking about: where were they held?'

'The last one was at Caxton Hall,' she said, giving me an expectant glance.

'How far back?'

'About this time last year. The next one must be – '

'And was that when your husband pointed me out?'

'If it was you,' she said with a renewal of caution.

The whole of Goddard Street had been newly redeveloped with twin cliff-faces of tinted glass and plastics, housing companies with names like Parker Enterprises and Smith's Metal Rods. Alongside one of the more modest entrances was a plaque bearing the words: 'Dobbs & Terry, Commercial and Industrial Consultants.' Guiding me into the building, Mrs Cotter led the way into a self-service lift and after a number of false starts elevated us to the third floor and a carpeted outer office where she delivered a woman-to-woman smile to a round-faced, bespectacled girl wearing a cherry-red jersey and a gold necklet. 'Is my long-suffering husband available, Wendy? Tell him I'd like to see him for just a moment, there's a love.'

As we waited I said, 'This must seem slightly weird

to you. But you could be doing me a bigger favour than you know.'

'I hope so. It's dreadful to have a memory lapse like that. A friend of mine – Oh, Maurice, there you are.'

From a nearby door had emerged a short, rotund individual whose enormous, thick-rimmed glasses concealed much of a shiny face. He looked rather older than his wife: middle forties, I estimated. While she was explaining matters to him I carried out a careful survey. His appearance struck no specific bell; on the other hand, it seemed to me not impossible that I had known him in a superficial way at some time. He was the type that one can meet and subsequently forget, and then meet and forget again; like a small-part character actor who passes out of mind between appearances. Having listened attentively to what she told him, he turned to me with an engaging anxiety to oblige.

'Caxton Hall last year,' he repeated. There was a trace of a Lancashire dialect. 'I seem to remember . . . that's right, yes, I did point you out to my wife. At least if it wasn't you it was someone extremely . . . Mr Thomas, isn't it?'

'Charles Thomas,' I agreed, 'as far as I know.'

'Hm. We'd been introduced the year before. Lost your memory, you say?'

'Something like that. Do you know anything about me?'

He cogitated, removing the glasses to inspect me with small watery eyes. 'As I understood it, you were acting in some kind of free-lance capacity for an industrial advisory set-up. Must confess I don't recall its name.'

'Did we talk?'

'Not last year. I was going to come across for a word, but you went before I had a chance. The previous year we had quite a chat.' He squeezed his little eyes. 'Die-stamping equipment.'

'Oh yes?'

I thought about it. I found I knew something about die-stamping equipment: quite a lot, in fact. Trying to associate the topic with Maurice Cotter was a different matter. He and his wife were watching me concernedly. 'That seems feasible,' I informed them. 'Though I must be honest and say I've no recollection at all of our meeting. You're positive it was me?'

'I've a reasonably good memory for faces.' He sounded doubtful.

'It's funny,' put in his wife, 'that it should strike me as well.'

'Seems fairly conclusive,' I agreed. 'Anything else about Charles Thomas come back to you? Home address, for instance?'

'Ah. There you've got me.' Cotter looked sincerely grieved. 'I'm afraid you were just a – a conference contact, if I can put it like that. And as for the other people I was with at the time – '

'There can't be that many industrial advisory bodies,' interposed his wife. 'Mightn't it be worth checking with them all, see if one knows about you?'

I nodded. 'Good idea.'

'And if you draw blank there,' added Cotter, hooking his glasses back on to his fleshy ears, 'how about popping along to the police, giving them your name and asking them to trace any family? They're pretty good, you know. They'll help you like a shot.'

'Of course they will. What a relief,' I said heartily, 'to have something to go on. I'm tremendously grateful to you both. I'll shove off now and see what I can do.'

'Good luck,' they chorused. Cotter added, 'When you've managed to find yourself – ha, ha – do come back and tell us about it. We'll be most interested to hear.'

By the time I had reached a vacant callbox it was nearly six-thirty. There were two D. F. Clarks in the local directory, but one lived in Hampstead Village. I dialled the number of the other. When the receiver was picked up, the pips began immediately so that I couldn't hear whether the voice was male or female. I pushed in twopence. The voice was male. 'Douglas Clark speaking.'

'Is Mrs Clark there?'

'Who is it?'

The voice was peremptory. On a semi-official note I said, 'Parkins Brothers, The Broadway.' There was a baffled pause.

'Hold the line.'

Sally came on in equal mystification. 'Who's this?'

'Keep your voice normal.' I spoke quietly. 'It's John – John Tiverton, the real or the imagined; I'm still not sure which. Sorry, but I had to phone. Say "Oh yes" or something.'

'Oh yes,' she said in a tone of cool enlightenment.

'I told Doug – your husband – that I was Parkins Brothers.'

'That's fine, then, thank you.'

'I only want to ask you something. Does the name Charles Thomas mean anything to you?'

A marginal pause.

'No, not a thing, thank you.'

'Think hard. It's very important.'

'Just a moment. Darling . . .' Her voice became muffled. 'Will you be a pet and glance in the freezer and see if there are two chickens or only one?' She returned to me, speaking softly. 'Who's this Charles Thomas supposed to be?'

'An industrial consultant of some kind. You've not heard of him?'

'Not consciously. But then it's hardly an ear-grabbing name, is it? You might try it on Mel Simpson. He was always having contacts with people like that.'

'Okay, Sally. Thanks.'

'Two?' she asked. 'I have two in stock, so I shan't be needing any more. Thank you for calling. Bye.'

I placed the receiver down. Leaning against the directory rack, I gazed down the street, feeling the slow advance of a kind of gentle panic. A choice of thread-ends seemed to confront me: unless I grasped them in the correct order, some edifice would shiver and topple, engulfing me in a rubble mass from which no escape would be possible. I looked at my watch. It was now twenty to seven.

The temptation was to head straight on; but physical debility was again clawing at me and I knew I must eat. Between leaving Kaltmans and visiting Sally I had consumed a chocolate bar in the reading-room of a branch library: there had been no time for anything else. Leaving the callbox, I wandered towards a parade of shops until I found a coffee bar where I bought a cheese roll and some wrapped chocolate wafers, swallowing them with a cupful of a beverage which might with equal legitimacy have passed for coffee, tea, drinking chocolate or thin soup. The place was full of busmen. A late evening newspaper had been left on a stool at the counter; I glanced through it, but there was nothing of significance. I forced myself to sit on for another five minutes. Then I left, heading for the bus terminus.

CHAPTER 15

Locating Phillison's house in Edgware proved tricky. I remembered the name of the street but not the number, and so I had to ask at several doors until I found someone who had heard of him. When I arrived, I rested briefly before ringing.

Phillison himself came to the door. He was a bachelor, but I had assumed him to have a housekeeper.

'Hullo,' I said.

The disappointment had a dull edge to it by now. He peered out at me, moving aside so that the hall light shone on my features. 'Good evening,' he said courteously. 'Not from the Conservative Party, are you? I sent my sub-scription by post.'

'Nothing political,' I assured him. 'I wonder if you can spare time for a quick word, Mr Phillison? My name's Thomas.'

'Yes?' He remained urbane, but I thought I detected a faint stiffening of his frame. 'Perhaps you'd care to step inside,' he suggested after a moment.

In the hall we faced one another. The house, which had an outer shell of mock-Tudor, was a model of mid-wars tattiness inside, with woodwork painted a matt brown. It had that musty-sweet odour which seems to collect in the homes of those who live alone. Phillison was clad in a beige woollen waistcoat that sagged at the lapels, baggy fawn trousers and carpet slippers. I said, 'I'm sorry to disturb you, but it was rather – '

'Not in the least. Mr . . . Thomas, you said?'

I returned his inspection. 'Charles Thomas. Possibly

you've heard of me?'

With the tip of a fingernail he scratched the lobe of an ear. 'I'm so sorry. Ought I have?'

The hall light was low-wattage, masked by a shade. He inched forward as though trying to examine me more narrowly without appearing rude; then stepped back. 'Do come through to the lounge, won't you?'

It was a quaintly old-fashioned word for the starkest of living-rooms at the rear of the house. A couple of hard-looking easy chairs flanked a single-bar electric fire standing on an archaic hearth; on the other side of the room was a table covered by a green baize cloth on which were strewn numerous pamphlets and sheets of paper; there were three upright leather chairs in odd places, facing different ways; the floor was concealed by a carpet which would have looked desperately inadequate in a slum basement. The electric fire was out. Apparently oblivious of the surroundings and the temperature, Phillison rested a thigh on an edge of the table and kept up his inspection while I stood as close as possible to the back of one of the easy chairs, yearning for an invitation to sit.

Outside the lab environment and without his working smock, he looked like another man. Remote still, and yet astute, regarding me with an indefinable air of appraisal that I found unnerving. I said, 'This may sound like a silly question, but have we met before?'

He cleared his throat. 'I'm just giving that some thought.'

'The answer's vital.' I looked at him steadily. 'You see, I know you. You're Tony Phillison and you work at Kaltmans in the research section. You specialize in metal fatigue.'

Relaxation crept into his stance. He lowered the other

side of himself to the table.

'Ah,' he observed. 'That's a little better.'

He sat surveying me, still with vestiges of reserve.

'What's better?' I asked.

'The fact that you appreciate my difficulty. One doesn't like to blunder in regardless.'

'Naturally not.' I wrestled for something to say that might spark a coherent reply. 'Of course, you know all there is to know about John Tiverton?'

He looked down at the tattered carpet for a considerable time; then back towards me, but not directly at my face.

'Puts me in something of a dilemma,' he said delicately. 'You see, I – well, the names alone ought to be clinchers, I dare say. But when all's said and done, there's not been a great deal of visual approach. You'd agree there?'

'Possibly,' I said cautiously.

'Which throws me in the position of having to take certain things on trust. Don't think I'm imputing anything. But would you object if we delved a fraction deeper into the question of bona fides?'

'I wouldn't object in the slightest.'

Folding his wool-sheathed arms, he looked me up and down. 'You see, there's only twice been what you might term visual contact. Twice exactly. If you like I can specify the occasions. Once at the window of – a certain office window, in a somewhat poor light: the second time in the back seat of a taxi, from the pavement.' He raised his chin at me. 'Not a lot, is it? Hardly the face-spotters' dream. Just the same, on certain conditions I'm prepared to accept . . .'

Plucking up a pamphlet from the table, he fingered it, eyed the print, put it down. 'Tell me this: does he know you're here, or have you come under your own steam, as it were?'

'Tiverton?' I queried.

He squinted, puzzled. 'Well, all right. Play it that way if you prefer. It's a point of reference, I suppose. I only asked, because it struck me there could be a slight hazard involved.'

'Why?' I was keeping the questions brief: they seemed sufficient to maintain him at tickover, and at any moment he might slip into explanatory top gear.

'Why?' he repeated as though testing the syllable for structural deformity. 'Well, I'm not supposed to come into this, am I? Not overtly. I'm the fixer-up, the maker of the arrangements. That was the understanding. Stay in the background, were my orders: keep a low profile. Now here you are, bearding me in my den, if you'll forgive the expression. Granted it's a dark night and I'm sure you're confident of your powers to travel incognito, but the fact remains . . .'

Abstractedly for a while he strummed his lower lip with a finger before resuming. 'I expect you'd like me to stop rattling on. You must excuse my apparent absorption with my own security. I've a lot at stake, you see, on a personal basis. A lot to lose. Anyway . . .' With conscious bravery he waved this aside. 'What can I do to help?'

My brain stagnated. His expression now was one of resolute attentiveness: he was waiting for me to tell him how he could assist. I uttered the first words that strayed into my head. 'I must contact Mel Simpson.'

For several seconds he remained mute. Without visible alteration, his manner contrived to convey an extra dimension of perplexity. I rested my forearms on the chair-back, partly for effect but chiefly because it was becoming impossible to stand unsupported. Phillison's fish-gaze wavered. Reclaiming the pamphlet, he folded it precisely double and then double again, stropping the creases with neat small journeys of finger and thumb.

'You'll pardon my asking,' he said, sounding none too sure about it, 'but I was under the impression you had good contact? I mean, it was surely never intended – '

'The best of contacts can separate now and then.' His downbeat reaction had increased my confidence. 'It's urgent that I see him, and routine lines have proved negative. That's why I came to you.'

'But I can't authorize an off-limits approach. You know that.'

'I'm not asking you to authorize anything. Just tell me where he is, if you know.'

'At home, probably, by now,' Phillison said unhappily.

'And where's that?'

He doubled the pamphlet yet again. 'You don't have his home address? In that case I could hardly – '

'Security,' I explained.

'Quite; which is the reason I can't – '

'Don't you understand?' I made my leaning posture slightly more cavalier. 'Routine and standby connections have let me down. Something's happened that he has to know about – fast.'

He considered this, his facial skin forming folds and puckers of acute dubiety.

'If you're Thomas – ' he began.

'You seem to take a lot of convincing.'

He allowed himself a faint smile. 'In my position that's inevitable. The percentage game is what I deal in.'

'Unless you put me in touch with Simpson,' I said deliberately, 'the percentage for you isn't going to look too healthy.'

Agitation seized him. 'I'm in an impossible position. I can't have people coming here and . . . For all I know, this other crowd could be having the place watched. Twenty-four hours a day. The works. I'm not briefed for a situation where somebody calls and says he's Thomas and looks enough like him to half-persuade me and then demands – '

'What are you briefed for?'

I kept my voice sharp. He stared across in a hunted manner before returning to the solace of his pamphlet, now a quadrupled disc which he was pulverizing between the bases of his palms with a nervous compulsiveness.

'Just the operational mechanics. That's my function, always has been. Both sides know that. Every deal needs a link man. That's me.'

'So link me with Simpson.' I seated myself in the chair.

'Suppose I said he's not reachable?'

I rested my head. 'I wouldn't believe you.'

Discarding the mangled pamphlet, he left the table and started to prowl. 'Do I smell a rat?' he asked presently, his voice querulously high. 'Some kind of security check before the deal goes through . . . is that it? Because if it is, I can assure you you're wasting your time. I repeat, I've too much at stake to play doubles and triples . . .'

'Me too.'

'Yes, well, I agree it represents an enormous step for you and you want to safeguard your own interests as far as you can: that's entirely understandable. You could be running your neck into a noose. What I don't understand is this Simpson angle. If he wanted to check up on me – '

'He doesn't,' I said tiredly. 'I've got to speak to him, that's all. Before tomorrow.'

Phillison came to a standstill between me and the window. It was a multi-paned affair with a length of plain mustard-coloured curtaining suspended limply on either side; part of one of them had left the rail. He was one of these people who see nothing immediately about them; one wonders to what end their infinite labours to feather their own nests are directed, when neither nests nor feathers are of the least importance to them.

'I'll call Simpson,' he said.

I stood at his shoulder as he dialled. Although he did his best to hide the digits, I could see that the number he was calling was the genuine one. The ringing tone commenced. I kept my left ear close to the receiver. A click was followed by Simpson's unmistakable purr.

'Three-seven-five-nine.'

'Phillison here, sir. So sorry to trouble you after hours. Just a small matter that's come up. Thought I'd better let you know about it.'

'Yes, Tony?'

There was no impatience in the phrase; it was lobbed in like a blob of grease to assist free running.

'It concerns Mr McKenzie. Seems he's been trying to reach you with a view to clarifying a few points on the alternator contract.'

'Oh yes?' Superficially the voice at the other end was the same. The delivery, however, was fractionally slower, betraying a new alertness.

'Only you've not been available. It's slightly urgent, I understand, because Mr McKenzie has to talk to his board tomorrow and is anxious to clear up the outstanding factors.'

'Of course. But I thought he had my phone number?'

'Not your home one, sir, apparently.'

A small interval elapsed. I visualized Simpson staring past the receiver at one of his framed originals, his mind galloping like the racing thoroughbreds they depicted. When he spoke again the enunciation was slower than ever and very distinct. 'When did Mr McKenzie tell you this?'

'Just a few moments ago.'

'By phone?'

'No, sir. In person.'

A further pause. 'I see. Is he there with you now?'

'Yes, he is.'

'Would you mind asking him to wait while I go and arm myself with the folder? Luckily I brought it home with me this evening. Don't hold on, I'll call you back.'

'Very good, sir.' Phillison hung up.

'Prudent of him,' I said.

'Wouldn't you have done the same?'

'If I were in his line of country.'

His eyebrows twitched. 'I understood you were.'

'On the fringe,' I said, wondering what we were talking about.

He appeared satisfied. 'A good many fringe people in the world,' he observed, employing a forefinger to rub some coagulated dust off the telephone dial. 'Some might regard me as one. It's all a question of definition. If you take as a yardstick – '

The phone rang. His hand darted towards it; before lifting the receiver he waited for a few more rings, finally making the action a measured one. He spoke temperately. 'Phillison here.'

'Mel Simpson, Tony. I'm now equipped for dealing with Mr McKenzie's inquiries. But it strikes me: he might prefer a face-to-face. Awkward, dealing in figures over the blower. Ask him if he'd like a rendezvous.'

Phillison lowered the mouthpiece. 'Mr Simpson wonders – '

'I heard. And I certainly would, tell him.'

'That would suit Mr McKenzie very well,' Phillison

said smoothly into the line. 'Where shall he make for?'

'The Hound and Bugle. It's the northern end of West Hendon, at the junction of – '

'I know it, sir. I'm sure Mr McKenzie does, but I can direct him if not.'

'Ask him to wait for me in the North Way Lounge and to get himself a drink at my expense.' Simpson coughed. 'I may be held up slightly, but tell him I'll be along as soon as possible.'

CHAPTER 16

The popular bars evidently were the saloon and the Snug, the latter's dimensions running counter to its titular description, as I discovered on my way in by walking through the wrong door. The North Way Lounge at the back of the roadhouse was contrastingly cool, detached, finely appointed, furnished with tables of polished wood and seats unholstered in what looked like pigskin, superior in every way, and almost deserted. A glance told me that I was there before Simpson. Nobody was behind the bar. I set out on the substantial walk to reach it, picking my feet out of boglike carpet at every stride.

The bar surround was encased in bulbous black leather that blended discreetly with the grained oak and chrome. I tapped the small bell provided. Presently from a doorway connecting the North Way with the Snug appeared a stately barman with sideboards reaching almost to his jawline. 'Sorry to have kept you waiting, sir,' he announced with a penitence that seemed excessive.

His movements as he served me with a large scotch and ginger were measured but efficient. I carried the drink to a corner table. After a survey of the lounge, in the manner of a captain from the bridge, he paced back into the animation next door.

Only one other table in the lounge was occupied. Two men were in conversation over half-pints; there was a mood of tranquillity about them, as though they were in exclusive occupation of some private club in the hour before dinner. Both were young and earnest, with things to discuss. Everyday things. Anger thrust itself again to the surface as I watched them. Why me? Why did it have to be me?

To divert my mind I thought back over the encounter with Phillison. On an empty stomach my mental processes were keener. My conclusion was that, although I had learned nothing from our exchanges, there was plenty that could be deduced. Echoes from the meeting came at me like bullets to be taken aside for ballistic tests.

What are you briefed for? Just the operational mechanics. Every deal needs a link man. You could be running your neck into a noose. I'm the fixer-up, the maker of the arrangements . . . Something had been arranged. In a sense, this was reassuring, indicating that I was not adrift in a tideless sea; but the reassurance remained valid only if I could pinpoint its root, and do so without inordinate delay: another day like this would kill me.

Phillison had arranged something. This was more promising. Phillison had fixed up something in conjunction with Simpson, who was my chief. John Tiverton's chief? Or Charles Thomas's? Ignore that for the moment. No, it couldn't be ignored, because it was fundamental to the whole enigma. *Play it that way if you like. It's a point of reference.* For whom? All three of us? Four of us?

I drank some whisky. One of the earnest young men rose and walked to the toilet door; the other took up an

Evening Standard. Briefly I listened to the vocal buzz from the Snug.

How widespread could a conspiracy be? It would have to embrace everybody. Family, neighbours, colleagues. Could it be done? Would it be? The answer to both questions was beyond dispute. In scientific research, one practised the art of the theoretically feasible: sometimes it was difficult to define the area in which it merged into the blind alley of the impracticable, although even here there was occasionally a side-passage providing a way out. But this? Reason rebelled.

Therefore, failing some miracle of plastic surgery, I was not John Tiverton. I was Charles Thomas. If the testimony of the Cotters had not been enough, there was the fact that it was the name which had come automatically to my lips at Mrs Carpenter's hotel. Phillison had known it, too. As near as made no difference, he had known me. Even though he had, on his own admission, glimpsed me only twice: once in a taxi, another time against a window.

An office window. Simpson's office? In a dim light. This suggested evening. Why should Phillison have seen me fleetingly in Simpson's room at Kaltmans on a solitary occasion after normal hours? What had I, Charles Thomas, been doing there if I was known to nobody else in the building?

A figure lowered itself into the chair opposite me. 'I'll have the same, I think,' said Simpson.

He had not approached through the swing doors at the end of the lounge. I looked round; the toilet door was still shuddering slightly. He said, 'I had to be sure it was you. Feel like doing the honours?'

I went and thumped the bell at the bar. The bartender returned; while he was pouring the measure I saw the young man emerge from the toilet and rejoin his companion at their table. They began talking again.

'Thanks,' Simpson said politely. 'Here's to everything.'

'I'd second the proposition,' I told him, 'if I knew what anything was.'

Setting his glass down with a soft thump, he leaned forward. 'What makes you say that?'

'Fatigue,' I ventured.

He fingered the stem of the glass. 'Exhaustion? Is this what you're saying?'

Not knowing what else to do, I shrugged. 'I'm pretty tired.'

'You were fine a week ago.'

His voice was sharp, not angrily so but as though he was tensed-up about something. I ran a hand wearily through my hair. 'I've been trying to get things sorted out in my mind . . .'

'Tiny bit late for that, isn't it?' He took an edgy gulp of whisky. 'Is this what you went to Phillison about? Why the blazes go to him, anyhow? I was available on the usual link.'

'I didn't think you were.'

He stared. 'You must be far gone. Don't crack up on us, will you?'

'I'm not sure it hasn't happened already.'

He lowered his glass, this time carefully so that it met the table without a sound. Keeping both hands upon it for a moment, he slid them suddenly across the glossed surface and clasped them under my chin, bringing across the upper part of his body until his face was within a foot of mine.

'Look: what is this? Has anyone got at you? Not trying to raise your price, by any chance?'

My return stare gave nothing away. 'Because I can tell you,' he went on softly, 'the deal you got was the most we could offer – as I explained at the time. You accepted. Now you come to me – or rather you go to Phillison, of all the damn fool capers – talking about feeling tired and cracking up, as though you expect me to respond with balm and consolation on the spot, when you must realize . . .' He paused, evidently hit by a thought. 'Am I talking out of turn?' he asked in a new voice, quieter still. 'Not in danger, are you?'

'I'm not sure.'

'Why, what's happened?'

'I met someone today,' I said, watching him, 'who recognized me.'

'As Thomas, you mean?'

I nodded. He said quickly, 'It needn't matter . . . we agreed there was always that chance. Who was it?'

'A professional associate. Name of Cotter.'

'Cotter?' He frowned at the table. 'Maurice Cotter, of Dobbs and Terry? Couldn't you have kept out of his way?'

'I came on him unexpectedly. Anyway we'd only met a couple of times before – I hardly remembered him.'

'But he remembered you?'

'Apparently we had a chat a year or two ago. I must have forgotten.'

Simpson seemed absorbed in mental calculations. 'Cotter's harmless,' he announced at last. 'The original amiable fool. If he does blab about it, nobody will take much notice. This all that was bothering you?'

'Apart from the crash.'

He stiffened. 'What are you getting at now?'

'Reading the Press report of my untimely demise – '

'Tiverton's, you mean?'

I sat back, removing my face from the uncomfortable proximity of his probing eyeballs. 'That's just it,' I said, slightly breathless. My brain had run dry of evasions: I could think of no other way of putting the case than to put it. 'After reading what it said, I started trying to work things out. The more I thought about it, the more confused I got. This is what I meant about . . . about cracking up. Mel, I'm worried. I can't sort myself out any more. What's happened to me? Am I Tiverton or Thomas?'

While I was speaking, his eyes had steadily been acquiring the circular geometry that reminded me of a famous comedian whom I had once witnessed, in cinematic close-up, hearing the news that he had been drafted into the US Army. But there was no comedy in Simpson's voice.

'Jesus *Christ*,' he said on an outward breath.

During the succeeding interlude there was time for me to observe that the young men at the other table had apparently concluded their talk. One had returned to the *Standard*; the other was clasping his half-pint tankard and gazing idly at the bar.

Simpson sat back; then advanced again, moistening his lips with his tongue. His voice was low-pitched but weighty.

'You did right to get in touch. How long have you felt like this?'

'Past couple of days.'

'Now listen. You're tired, you say. Let's take it from there. You've been working too hard at this? Maybe that's not the word . . . Too whole-heartedly? It's a danger that hadn't occurred to either of us, but I can quite see – '

'For God's sake.' My own voice sounded like a hiss. 'Don't you understand what I'm saying? Working at what? Is there something I'm meant to be doing that nobody else should know about?'

Restraint stole into his attitude. His scrutiny was as intense as ever, but to it was now added an element of reserve, akin to Phillison's. 'Go on,' he said.

'How can I go on? I'm lost. I'm groping in the dark and nobody will switch a light on. That's why I had to talk to you.'

'But you haven't talked. Not sensibly. I still can't make out . . . Are you asking for a re-briefing?'

I peered at him. 'If you like.'

'It's not what I like. I just want to help. You seem to have got yourself into a rare old state about the thing, but assuming – '

'What thing?'

Once more Simpson sat back, this time with an air of finality. He studied me broodingly.

'Tell me,' he requested, 'did something occur to throw you off-beam – something specific? Just now you mentioned the crash. You were re-reading the report. What about it?'

'Was it genuine?'

'The report? Why shouldn't it have been? They never – '

'The crash.'

Anger sparkled in his pupils. 'Just what are you imputing? Some kind of treble-cross?'

'All I'm trying to get at – '

'It must have occurred to you that if there had been no crash, none of this would have been necessary. Why on earth should we fabricate that?'

I said desperately, 'This is part of what I can't fathom. Was I – was Tiverton killed that night?'

'Not at once, but he died later. I told you.'

'Then I'm Charles Thomas?'

He seemed speechless. After a while he said tentatively, 'I think I'm beginning to see. You're like a TV star in a long-running serial . . . the part starts to take him over. Is this the way you feel?'

'So I'm acting a part?'

'Isn't this what we agreed you musn't do?' He gazed at me as though confident that this made everything crystal-clear. When he saw that it didn't, he looked a worried man. 'Christ,' he said again, 'you must have gone at it too hard. You need a break. A total halt for a week at least. Will that do it, would you think?'

'What,' I said patiently, 'have I gone too hard at?'

He placed the knuckle of his right hand against his mouth and pondered for a moment. 'How old is Barbara?' he asked suddenly.

'Seven.'

'Date of birth?'

'Sixteenth of March, sixty-nine.'

'Michael?'

'November nine, seventy-two.'

'Where did you marry Valerie?'

'Croydon Register Office.'

'Who was there?'

I reeled off some names. He watched me narrowly; as I finished he gave a slow nod. 'You're all right,' he said. 'What are the special properties of LVG under conditions of ultra-high temperature and extreme stress?'

I told him. In detail. His response was to put another technical question, a more complex one: my reply was in full flood when he interrupted. 'I don't get it,' he said, frowning. 'You don't seem confused. It's all at your fingertips. What's the problem?'

'I don't know who I am.'

He gave another nod. A decision seemed to have been

arrived at. 'Well,' he said briskly, 'you're John Tiverton, of course.'

'Then why didn't Val know me? Joan, Theobald, any of them?'

'Wait a bit.' He spoke with a resumption of wariness. 'What do you mean, why didn't they . . . When was this?'

'Yesterday and today. I've been driven out of my mind, trying to – '

'God in heaven.' Simpson had come upright in his chair. 'What have you done? You haven't blown it?'

'How do I know?' I was on my feet, shouting at him. 'How can I possibly know, if no one will tell me?'

My thump on the table toppled both whisky glasses, sent them rolling until they fell intact into the carpet. I stamped on the nearer, driving the fragments deeper into the pile. 'You're going to have to level with me, Mel Simpson. I can't take any more of this. It's sending me crazy. Can't you see the condition I'm in?'

'Yes,' he said quietly. 'I think I can see that very well.'

I became conscious of a presence at my left shoulder. Turning, I looked into a pair of cold grey eyes. They belonged to the stockier of the two young men from the other table. His leaner companion had his back to the swing doors of the lounge: he was watching us impassively.

Simpson came to his feet. 'Better come along with us, old man.' He spoke soothingly, shuffling the glass splinters beneath the table with a side-footed action. 'I can tell you're not a hundred per cent by any means. We must get things sorted out.'

The stocky young man stood between me and the toilet door. With a shrug I rounded the table on Simpson's side.

'Fine by me,' I said submissively. 'I don't care what happens, just so long as I get the chance to put a few relevant questions that should help to – '

My run was timed to coincide with a slackening of their postures. The bar was about four feet high: I cleared it in two stages, my trailing right foot sweeping several tankards and a soda siphon in a clatter to the tiled floor behind. Beyond the dividing doorway, the stately barman was bearing three brimming schooners of sherry from the serving counter to a Snug customer; they flew in three directions as I thrust past, bringing from him a jerky 'Here, what the – ?' that was drowned in a raucous cheer as I rolled myself over the second barrier to land in a heap at the feet of the drinkers. Dragging myself up, I staggered towards the Snug door, roared on by the onlookers.

'Told you your prices were too steep, Harold,' yelled someone. The door, stiffly sprung, came back on me as I struggled through, turning my head at the last instant to catch sight of the leaner young man battling through the crowd towards me from the lounge doors.

Outside on the damp pavement I halted. There was a choice of three ways: left, right, or across the street to a side turning. The traffic helped me to decide. Wheeling left, I ran.

CHAPTER 17

Surfacing at Baker Street, I saw that they were still with me. Some way below on the escalator, staying within range but keeping their distance.

I reasoned that they would hardly risk trying to detain me in such a public place. More likely they would wait until I was incautious enough to stray from the main-stream.

A dilemma faced me. By staying with the crowd I also stayed with the bright lights, where pursuit was easier. The darker back streets offered more chance of eluding tactics; plus a greater risk of being cornered. Both the men were younger than myself, larger, physically more formidable in every way. And they were professionals. At the head of the escalator I stepped off rapidly, handing in my ticket and making a fast dive for a side exit.

Not fast enough. As I glanced back, the leader of the pair came gliding over the top, looking my way.

Baker Street itself was fiercely lit enough: it also happened to be virtually deserted. The handful of people who had left the Underground with me had dispersed through various exits. It was an intermediate time of evening, and not exactly one of London's hotspots. I wished I had kept on the train to Oxford Circus, but claustrophobia had been crawling up on me, shrinking the walls and ceiling of the Tube compartment, crushing them inwards and downwards until, losing my nerve, I had felt compelled to dive out and take my chance.

I set off southwards at a trot, alert for a cruising taxi.

Those that did come along were travelling at a uniform forty, enmeshed in the knots of traffic that surged spasmodically as the lights changed. Fifty yards to my rear, the two had emerged from the station and were following in fast strides.

For a moment I was baffled. Then it came to me. They didn't want to catch up with me here. They didn't necessarily want to catch up at all. What they were after was my destination.

Simpson was rattled. Whatever game he was playing, he still didn't know whether my evident departure from the rules was deliberate or inadvertent: he had to find out, and the best way of doing so was to keep tabs on me for a while. Reaching this conclusion, I slowed up to test it. A quick glance confirmed the theory. The pair had adjusted their pace to remain in arrears.

A kind of sneering anger erupted within me. It was the clumsiest of operations, worthier of one of those plotless television thrillers than of responsible men with enviable IQs. Okay, I thought. If they wanted it that way, they could have it.

At Oxford Street I turned right to Marble Arch, bearing right again into Edgware Road. Some distance along, a cinema was showing a film about teenage rebellion; the last screening had already begun. Entering the foyer, I bought a stalls ticket, walked through unhurriedly and was shown to an end-of-row seat a third of the way down.

Behind me there were movements, the tilting of seats. I guessed they were finding the best positions they could for keeping me in view. I made myself smile in the semi-darkness. The film looked terrible.

Shutting my eyes, I blotted out the sound and tried some more reasoning.

I was playing a part, only I wasn't playing a part. Whatever I was doing, I'd been overdoing. The fact that Valerie and the rest had been given the chance not to recognize me was somehow disastrous. I knew a good deal about metal alloys.

Phillison had spoken of 'this other crowd'.

A general conspiracy I had ruled out. This had steered me remorselessly to the conviction that I was, indeed, Charles Thomas; whoever he was.

And yet Simpson, under pressure, had averred that I was John Tiverton.

However, it had emerged too glibly, too pat. He had

said it in the manner of one seizing an opportunity, after
my unequivocal declaration that I didn't know who I was.
In other words, he was only too content that I should
believe myself to be Tiverton.

Why?

Because the real Tiverton was dead. And Simpson
didn't want him to be dead.

Why not?

Because he, Simpson, wanted to use him in some way.

But if I was Charles Thomas, why had I gone home the
previous day as John Tiverton, to be met on all sides by
stupefied blankness?

As before, I tried to throw my mind back an hour
earlier, to the period after I had left the library reading-
room and reached the street. Here was the gulf. Strive as
I might, I could recall nothing up to the moment I was
standing on my own doorstep – Tiverton's doorstep –
letting myself into the house. Here was the crucial phase,
the key to the cipher. If I could just carry myself back
. . .

The warmth of the cinema had begun to exert an
effect, joining forces with the whisky and the lack of
nourishment to induce an overwhelming desire for sleep.
To combat the impulse I opened my eyes to watch the
screen, but the action there, vast and violent, was hurtful
to my head. Another dilemma. With closed eyes I was
liable to nod off; to keep them open was to invite a
migraine. Claustrophobia mounted a new assault. In
an abrupt resurgence of panic I slid out of the seat to
stand momentarily at a loss in the gangway, incapable of
fixing a course of action.

The corner of an eye showed me one of the pair half-
risen in his seat, waiting to see what I would do.

I set off purposefully for the exit. It meant passing

within feet of them, but I kept my gaze ahead and in any case the gloom was thick. I reached the foyer to find it deserted: the ticket-seller had packed up and gone home. Marble flooring rang beneath my shoes as I crossed to the glass doors leading to the street.

Under the exterior canopy I paused. To my rear, other feet were clacking across the marble. Without looking round I began walking smartly back towards Marble Arch. I was halfway there when a bus grunted to a crawl in a traffic tangle nearly opposite me: without pausing to consider, I dodged out from the pavement in front of a hemmed-in car and jumped aboard the bus as it took off again, feeling a quiet exultation as it gathered pace.

Before occupying a front seat of the lower deck I took a glance back. In the centre of one of the longer seats at the rear, the slimmer of the pair was already installed, poker-faced as he searched a pocket for change.

Traffic in Park Lane was dense, a multiple flow that dulled the senses. Through the side window I watched it with a sensation of dreamy despair: my chest and stomach seemed to have been filled with a viscous cement. When the conductor approached, I merely held out a tenpenny piece, leaving it to him to decide on the length of ticket. He handed me several inches. All the time I kept observation on the vehicles about us: they were like a lifeline to which I was clinging, a barrier against, and yet a link with, the world of sanity and logic beyond the pavement lamp columns. A heavy goods vehicle came level with us on the nearside: for a moment or two the driver's profile, immobile and relaxed a couple of feet above, was directly in my line of vision, and I wondered where he was making for: south, perhaps, for one of the Channel ports, or west for Bristol. It didn't matter. I had no interest in his pro-

gramme; the interest I had was in keeping my brain
involved, feeding it ordinary questions and mundane
place-names in a bid to assure myself that all touch with
reality had not been lost. At Hyde Park Corner the lorry
kept on south towards Victoria while the bus plunged and
bucked on a hazardous course through conflicting torrents
to emerge finally into the shallows leading to Knightsbridge.

The left-hand side of the thoroughfare presented a series
of gaunt buildings culminating in the brooding mass of
the Albert Hall, where the bus stopped briefly. Too late,
I decided to get off; by the time I had made a move the
bus was travelling again, sweeping into the approach to
Kensington High Street where the lighted shop windows
looked sedate and stand-offish, not to say hostile. Here I
was on territory with which I was less than familiar.
And beyond this area lay the wilderness of Hammer-
smith, the impersonal highways out of the capital. Instead
of returning to my seat I touched the bell-cord and completed a tight-rope progression to the rear platform,
meeting nobody's eye, jumping off as the bus decelerated,
landing heavily on the kerbstone but keeping my feet.
A following taxi swerved elaborately to avoid me. As I
began to canter back the way we had come I heard the
application of its brakes, the slam of a door.

I kept at a jogtrot past the big stores, not glancing
behind until I was abreast of the main entrance to
Kensington Gardens. Then I saw that the two had joined
forces again. In a relaxed fashion they were hurrying,
keeping in orbit, not bothering even to go through the
motions of concealment: there was no point, we were tacitly
unanimous on that. Weirdly, a kind of bond had established itself between us: hastily-improvised rules were
being adhered to, as though transgression on either side

would have been somehow unBritish. In these circumstances, to proceed at the double seemed a profligate misuse of energy. I slowed to a brisk walk.

Before long I was back in the Albert Hall vicinity and there were people about me. An oncoming surge that originated, like a phalanx of soldier ants, from a single primary source: the glass-enclosed front entrance to the building. Progress became difficult. I was against the current: to minimize its force I struck inwards, skirting the base of the convex façade until, reaching the entrance steps, I found myself more immutably blocked than before. Forced to halt, I chanced a look over the heads from my elevated position on the second step and by sheer luck spotted them, together still, shoulder to shoulder in the crush, anxious looks on their faces as they craned to determine which way I had gone. On impulse I fought my way up the remaining steps and through the exit doors into the approach to the entrance hall, from which the flood of emergent concert-goers seemed almost impenetrable.

My hope was that I had completed the manoeuvre unobserved. But in any event I couldn't remain where I was: I had either to regain the street by means of the opposite doors, or get inside. To follow the erupting flow was the easier and therefore the obvious course; I chose the harder. I earned myself some black looks as I battled through, but I made it to the foot of the left-hand staircase inside and from there managed to reach more placid waters at the back of the foyer, where I paused again to take stock.

As far as I could see, I had not been followed; but they could well have been still in the process of cleaving a path. Among so many bobbing heads, the differentiation of a couple was a daunting task: if they arrived, I should have little warning. To each side of me lay the entrances

to corridors. Choosing the less thickly-populated, I began
to work my way along it, staying close to the right-hand
wall and murmuring constant apologies as figures loomed
and side-stepped and passed on. The corridor took me in
a leftward sweep past numerous doors, through which I
caught glimpses of the stage cluttered with untenanted
orchestral chairs and music-stands, as well as segments of
the auditorium where a few stragglers were collecting
garments and programmes before adding themselves to
the drift. After a while I halted and turned.

I was in difficulties: but then so, I prayed, were my
pursuers. The possibility remained that they had failed
to see me entering the hall. But assuming they had, they
must be unsure whether I had stayed at ground level or
mounted a staircase to one of the galleries. Most likely
they would have to split up.

On a further assumption, that they took opposite ways
along the corridor I was in, they would ultimately meet
in a pincer movement on the far side. I didn't fancy
being the nail-head. A few yards along was a door;
making for it, I descended some stairs into the auditorium
towards the arena. I had in mind a traverse of the giant
interior and an exit by means of a different door that I
could see on the far side, with a knot of people squeezing
themselves into the bottleneck.

A uniformed official met me on the way down. 'Closing
the doors in three minutes,' he said fussily.

I said, 'I think I dropped a cigarette lighter.'

'Where was you sitting, sir?' He was a small, self-
important individual with a tiny trimmed moustache.

'Somewhere over there.' I pointed vaguely. 'Row J,
I think.'

'Wot number?'

He repeated the question as I stood gazing past his

left ear. I said, 'Oh . . . seventeen, I believe.' Someone
had entered the auditorium through a door to the right
of the choir stalls: someone tall and lean and youthful.
'I've lost the ticket, I'm afraid.'

Clicking his tongue, he began peering at the row
lettering. I added, 'It might have been farther over
than this,' and set off along a cross-gangway that led in a
gentle curve towards the curtained boxes on the far side.
The figure alongside the choir stalls had begun a hasty
descent of the steps that would bring him past the platform
into the arena. I lengthened my stride. Behind me the
official's voice called irritably.

'You won't find no row J over there, you know.'

Ignoring him, I struck upwards towards yet another
door that would take me back into the corridor from which
I had come. A face appeared in the opening. The eyes
looking down at me were cold. I veered, bearing to my
left again between two rows of seats, stumbling over one
that had not been upturned, finally reaching the next
gangway and climbing once more until I reached the
ornate base of one of the boxes. From the middle of the
arena came an echoing clash, followed by a shout from
the official.

'Where d'you think you're making for, might I ask?'

Without a pause I swung myself into the box, leapt the
seats and emerged via the open door at the rear opposite
a staircase. To my right was the thud-thud of rapid
footsteps. The stairs carried me in a series of exhausting
flights to the corridor at the back of the first gallery. By
now I had lost all sense of direction: I was simply running.
It occurred to me that I was travelling in a right-hand
sweep, which meant I was tracking back towards the
main entrance and therefore the residue of the departing

crowd, if any existed.

It seemed the best course. But the opposition had forestalled me, as I saw when I rounded the first bend of the staircase leading down into the foyer: the leaner one had got back fast from the arena to station himself at the doors, through which a trickle of the audience was still escaping. Mercifully he was looking the other way as I showed myself. I had time to withdraw, to return to the upper corridor and strike out along it in the reverse direction, hoping that my second pursuer was still looking for me in the region of the boxes on the lower level.

The building by now was becoming silent. The vague remote hum of people's voices had dipped to nothing: I was treading through a vacuum, a curvature in space. Obsessed with this image, I took no account of the sound my own footfalls were producing until the moment when a figure emerged swiftly from a side door to seize my arm.

I reacted with a frightened swing of the body that sent him against the wall. ''Ere!' he said indignantly, rubbing himself. 'We don't want none of that. What you after?'

I said, 'I want to get out.'

'Thought you was looking for a lighter.' He glared at me suspiciously, his minute moustache convulsing slightly with the workings of his mouth. 'If you want to leave, it's this way.' He pointed imperiously.

In automatic obedience I turned, just as the sound of advancing footsteps reached us from beyond the bend in the corridor. The official scowled. 'Some other bleeder now,' he muttered. 'All over the shop tonight . . . wot you all up to? Place is meant to be shut by now. If you can't – Hey! It's this way, I said . . .'

My sprint took me out of his view in seconds. Heedless of the noise, I continued at a run until I reached a doorway which I judged to be at a point directly opposite the main entrance in Kensington Road; diving through it, I clattered downstairs, past a closed buffet and into a kind of lobby where a group of about a dozen people, men and women, were shrugging themselves into coats and scarves. My arrival went practically unnoticed: a great deal of boisterous talk and laughter was in spate as the leading couples began to move towards an exit door.

As unobtrusively as possible I attached myself to those at the rear, several of whom were extremely large, drum-voiced men who continued to boom at each other across my head as I kept pace with them down a few steps to the lamplit pavement. A glance back showed me that we had emerged by door 13 on the south side of the hall, facing the broad steps leading down to Prince Consort Road. Without any particular design on my part, elements of the party closed up behind me as we crossed the road towards them; they seemed unaware that I was not of their number. One of them actually addressed a remark to me: something about 'Berlioz and his damned jottings' to which I returned enthusiastic assent, keeping my head down and adjusting my pace to stay in position.

At the foot of the steps we swept left, coming out presently into Exhibition Road where we turned right. The party's progress downhill in the direction of Cromwell Road was nerve-rackingly slow; the desire to break free of them, to forge ahead, was enormous. I put up stubborn resistance. For as long as my presence was accepted, it was the safest place; or so I hoped. There was no way of looking back to assess the position.

Ahead of me the group was stringing out. The leaders were humming part of the second movement of Mendelssohn's Italian Symphony, melodiously in time and tune; the man on my right was still declaiming against

Berlioz. After the second junction with a side road I began to shorten my stride, imperceptibly dropping back until I was the last in line, still with them but poised for take-off. I risked a backward glance.

The overhead lighting showed me empty pavements all the way back to the park.

I wanted to laugh. Pulling up, I rested a foot on a low wall beneath some railings and went through a pretence of retying the shoe lace, allowing the party to get well ahead. When there was fifty yards between us I checked again before crossing the road and proceeding in the same direction down to Cromwell Road. On the other side my rescue party, oblivious of both its augmentation and its depletion, continued in a loose-jointed crocodile towards Thurloe Square. I turned and headed east.

CHAPTER 18

'Is the room still available?' I asked.

'I said it would be.' There was an amused reproach in the dark eyes of Mrs Carpenter, lurking solicitude in the smile she turned on me as I faced her in the slim passage. The after-scent of multiple meals hung about us like spiced washing. 'How did you get on? Everything cleared up?'

'Cleared up?' I repeated blankly.

'The car and yourself. Did you go for an X-ray?'

'No, I didn't bother.' I made a grab for the table and hung on. 'There was a lot to be seen to.'

She was examining me without making it obvious. 'The room's all ready for you. What you need, I expect, is a good long sleep. Like a nightcap before you go up?'

The question was put casually, as though it was a social gesture and not a lifeline. Without pausing for a reply she went on, 'Come through to my den. There's a fire and it's quite cosy and we shouldn't be disturbed, unless they send a latecomer from the tourist office, in which case he'll be unlucky. Or she.' Her head tilted as she looked at me. 'Actually I was about to make coffee for myself. Like some?'

'I wouldn't say no.'

'Then say yes. Go inside and make yourself comfortable. I'll join you presently.'

The room had a pine ceiling and a fireplace of golden bricks in which smokeless fuel glowed like a vast molten ruby. Tightly-stocked bookshelves lined an entire wall. The other walls were papered in a pattern of silver-crowns on a white background. In addition to a television there was some costly stereo equipment. The armchair I fell backwards into received me with accommodating placidity, hissing slightly as the cushions compacted. Stretching my legs, I put my head back.

I was still in this position when she returned, producing a slight chinking of crockery as she arranged the tray on a small brass trolley next to the twin armchair on the other side of the rug. She sat, arriving neatly in an upright and yet relaxed position, sending me a schoolmarmish look from beneath her eyebrows as she lifted the coffee pot.

'White or black, Mr Thomas?'

'A touch of cream. Thank you.'

Reaching for the cup, I felt my head swim. Mrs Carpenter appeared to notice nothing wrong, although as I sat back I spilt coffee into the saucer and had to steady the cup with my other hand to prevent it tipping. Half-filling her own cup, she added a strong dilution of milk.

'This,' she remarked contentedly, 'is the one time of

the day when I cosset myself. No chance otherwise, what with meals to plan and laundry to check and people losing their door keys . . . I don't know.' The shake of her head expressed indulgence towards the human race in its frail entirety.

'You don't have any help?'

'Just a girl, Hilary, for the rooms. She buzzes off at six. Lives in at the YWCA in Fulham. After that I'm on my own.' She smiled brightly. 'I'm a widow, you see. Lost my husband four years ago. Up until then we ran the place together.'

I sipped at the coffee. 'You must find it hard work.'

'Keeps me out of mischief.' She eyed me across her cup. 'Are you married yourself?'

'I'm not sure.'

She laughed. 'Sounds indeterminate. Sorry . . . perhaps I shouldn't have asked.'

'No reason why you shouldn't.' Resting my cup on the chair-arm, I stared into the fire. 'But I'm really in no position to tell you at the moment, daft as it sounds.'

'You mean you've lost touch with your wife? You're not sure if she's alive?'

'Oh, she's alive.'

Touches of a frown appeared on the bridge of her nose. 'Then it's some sort of divorce mix-up, is it? One that's valid in another country but not here – that kind of thing?'

'Nothing like that.'

'I'm getting much too inquisitive,' she said after a pause. 'Occupational disease of landladies. You meet all these different people and you feel that unless you take an interest you're scarcely doing your job properly, but of course it's very hard to go on drawing the line between normal interest and nosiness. I have to admit – '

'It's myself,' I said abruptly.

'Pardon?'

'This – ' I tapped my head with a finger 'is where the confusion lies. I think I'm in some trouble – hell, I know I am. Only I'm not certain what it is.'

Mrs Carpenter looked suitably grave.

'Sounds to me as if that crash was worse than you tried to make out. Just a shake-up, you said. Are you quite sure you didn't hit your head? You haven't lost your memory? You'd much better say if you have. Believe me, you can't wander round London trying to – '

'Whether it's my memory that's gone I can't say. To my way of thinking, everything's blindingly clear. Or nearly everything.' I looked at her with a mixture of apology and defiance. 'None of it helps, though.'

I was prepared for her to rise with a murmured excuse and make for the telephone. She gave no sign of wanting to do so. Her gravity remained objective as she set down her cup and sat forward with hands folded on her trousered knees.

'I'd an idea there was something when you first arrived. Sort of a lost expression. Now tell me.' She became businesslike. 'This car crash of yours: firstly, are you positive it only happened yesterday, and secondly – '

'There was no car crash,' I said.

'No crash?'

'Not yesterday – not involving me. That was just a cover-up. Had to say something, didn't I? Turning up out of the blue, no luggage, looking dazed . . . I must have looked dazed. I was. I still am. If you knew what I'd been through . . .' I pondered her for a few moments. 'Care to hear about it?'

She rose. I waited resignedly for the discreet exit; but she merely came across to take my cup. 'Have some more coffee,' she said, pouring it, 'and start from the beginning.'

As she sat gazing into the anthracite radiance I was visited by the fear that she was busy with the manufacture of verbal sedatives. If so, I decided, I would leave her and go to bed. Telling her had been a help in its own right: a corner of the burden had been shifted an inch: I expected nothing more. But her first words jerked me out of this vein of thought.

'This notebook you mentioned. Have you still got it?'

Finding it in my inside pocket, I handed it across. 'If it means anything to you, then you're welcome to the damn thing. It looks like amateur shorthand. The kind that people work up for themselves to save a bit of time.'

'Or space,' she observed, perusing it. 'Or . . .' She hesitated.

'Or what?'

'Another purpose might be to prevent anyone else making head or tail of it.' She stared at one of the pages. 'Is it your handwriting?'

'Not certain. When it's just odd letters like that, it's hard to tell. Could I have it back a moment?'

She returned the notebook. 'What strikes me about this,' she resumed, 'is the logicality of it. No, wait. I mean that once you allow the basic premise – that you're not John Tiverton – virtually everything else that's happened is what *should* have happened. See my point? In other words, if we eliminate the fact that you were convinced of being Tiverton – simply wash it out – then we're left with a perfectly ordinary situation.'

'If that's the case, I'd hate to meet up with one that's abnormal. There's nothing – '

'Let me finish. What I'm saying is, something obviously occurred to make you think you were Tiverton – and once you did, of course the nightmare started.' She altered her position in the armchair. 'Are you fond of music?'

I was startled. With a glance at her stereophonic loudspeakers I said shortly, 'Yes, very. What has that to do with it?'

'I was only searching for a parallel. You see, it's like listening to a piece of music. If you hear the opening note of a phrase on the wrong beat, the rest of it makes no sense. Ever noticed that? If you're musical, you must have. There might be two of you, say, in a room, both listening to that same piece of music, and to one of you it's sublime and to the other it's a meaningless noise. But it's not the music at fault: it's the same music in each case. It's the listener who's got it wrong. With me?'

'So far. Can you lend me a pen?'

She produced one from her handbag. 'Now in your case,' she continued, passing it over, 'it seems to me you're in the position of the man who's missed that vital opening beat. Subsequent notes have been struck just as they ought to be, but to you they mean nothing.'

'Okay.' I was writing on a blank page of the notebook. 'Is this supposed to be a comfort?'

'To the extent that we can rule out some vast conspiracy – '

'I already have.'

' – and narrow it down to a reasonably confined one, involving your Melville Simpson and the Phillison creature and a couple of others. But if it's to go on making sense, we have to visualize an event that set you off on this Tiverton track and kept you there.' She reflected. 'Do you think it's possible he was a great friend of yours and your lives overlapped to such an extent that – '

'If they did, why should his wife be in the dark about me?'

'We can theorize about that later. For the moment let's stick to the basic thesis. Tiverton and you were friends, and he was killed. At the time of his death he was working on some tricky project for Kaltmans. You were the only one qualified to take over, so secretly Simpson roped you in . . .'

'Why secretly?'

'Some good reason,' she said patiently. 'The nature of the work, perhaps. He didn't want your involvement to leak out. Could it be . . .' Her pupils dilated. 'Might Tiverton's crash have been caused deliberately by some means? And he didn't want the same to happen to you?'

'Now you're talking.' I thumped the chair-arm with a fist.

'So, we have you treading in Tiverton's footsteps – driving yourself, possibly, to carry the work on. Overdoing it. Until finally, yesterday, something went snap! inside your brain and for a while you *became* Tiverton. It's possible, isn't it? Weirder cases than that are on record.'

'But how could I have known so much about him and his family? And why does no one at Kaltmans know me?'

'Because,' she said promptly, 'you've obviously been carrying out the work elsewhere. As for knowing all about him . . . I don't see that's so wonderful. It happens, doesn't it, with close friends? They tell one another everything. They even get personally involved. You see it a lot: especially with men, oddly enough.'

I went tiredly through the process of thinking in retrospect. Here and there, fragments of what she said fell clickingly into place, only to rattle around for lack of padding. I glanced down at the notebook. 'What do you think of this?' I asked.

She came over to study it with me. I had written: *Assuming I am Charles Thomas, who is Charles Thomas and what is his background?* I said, 'Ignore the message . . . compare the script. Does it strike you as being the same hand?'

She flicked back the pages. 'Could be,' she said dubiously. 'Jot down some hieroglyphics like these, just at random.'

The notebook was open at the page I had read before, with the word 'eggs' at the end of a baffling line. I inscribed a few letters in a similar style. She nodded. 'It might well be.'

My head dipped with weariness. 'If only someone would say, Yes, that's it – that's the answer. Instead of all this may be, might be . . . I can't take much more. If I'm not off my rocker already, the way I'm going – '

I was stopped by a double ring of the doorbell.

'Somebody after a room, no doubt.' Mrs Carpenter straightened to go outside.

'Hold it!'

I leapt up to place myself between her and the door. 'What if it's them?'

'The men who were after you?' She considered the matter before shaking her head. 'Most unlikely, I should say. Wouldn't they have rung before now?'

'They might have been calling up Simpson.'

'But I thought you'd given them the slip?'

'Hoped so. Can't be sure.' I kept my voice down. 'Look, do you often have people calling at this hour?'

'It does happen.' She took me gently by the arm. 'If you want to stay out of the way while I see who it is, why don't you pop downstairs to the kitchen? You know where to find it. You can stay there until they're out of the way.

If necessary – ' she gave me a rallying smile – 'you could hide in the store cupboard.'

'You won't let on I'm here?'

'As though I'd do such a thing.'

She sounded sincere. I had to trust her. The staircase to the semi-basement was in darkness; as I groped my way down I heard her footsteps overhead, clipping along the passage to the street door. In a panicky moment I tried to take the final stairs at a bound. Misjudging the treads, I missed my footing. The heel of my right shoe snagged the second stair from the bottom so that I was first pulled up, then shot forward in a sprawling dive.

My arms went out to break the impact, but before my hands connected with anything an explosion detonated itself on the crown of my skull.

Mrs Carpenter's face was a short distance from my eyes. She looked extremely concerned. I noticed that there was a light on. 'Put it out,' I advised stupidly. 'They'll be able to see.'

'It was just a young Canadian girl.' She was trying to raise me a little, prop me against the wall. 'She'd come to the wrong hotel – wanted Mason's along the street. Whatever happened to you?'

'Have I been out?'

'Like a stone, I should think. You were lying here when I came to look for you. Did you trip?'

Although I heard what she said, the cerebral tumult ruled out a reply. I felt that my eyes were starting from my sockets; for the time being there was nothing I could do to normalize them. Mrs Carpenter seemed to detect something. A look of excitement spread into her face. 'Something's come back?'

'By God it has.' I started to struggle up.

'Take it easy. We don't want you aggravating a

concussion. There might be – '

'To hell with concussion. It's cleared the blockage, don't you see? I knew it. I knew I'd get there. All it needed – '

'Wait a bit.' She was giving me support as we mounted the stairs. 'Let's get back to the living-room before you talk. Voices carry from here.'

When I was re-installed in the armchair before the fire she went to a dresser and poured brandy into a glass. 'Get that down you first,' she ordered.

She sat opposite me expectantly, giving the brass trolley next to her a dismissive thrust as though fearful that its continued presence might transport me back ten minutes, re-establishing the mental block. Brandy was the last thing I wanted, but I drank obediently. The delay was useful for sorting out the impressions and images and memories that were trickling back like wet sand through a sieve. Draining the glass, I placed it carefully on the carpet at the base of the chair, sat back in a hiss of cushions and matched the sound with a long, long breath of my own.

'You weren't so very far off the mark,' I told her.

CHAPTER 19

When Simpson got in touch with me on that May morning, I had been at a loose end for more than a week.

He sounded worried. 'Expect you're busy,' he said with a perfunctory observance of the niceties, 'but can you spare me an hour or two fairly soon? We've suffered a bombshell.'

From habit I said, 'I'll try to make it tomorrow.'

Operating free-lance as I did, I had cultivated the affectation of sounding less than immediately available; in the long run it was better for trade. Simpson wasn't fooled, but he played along politely. We had dealt with one another before.

At his request I drove to the region of the Kaltmans building in the late evening, parking my car out of sight in a nearby back street and completing the distance on foot. The kiosk at the main entrance was still manned at this hour, but, following instructions, I found my way to a side door to be admitted by Simpson personally, and he took me up to his office. He came instantly to the point.

'Our man Tiverton is dead,' he said.

'John Tiverton? The metallurgist?'

'Know of him?'

'Only that he was working on Backlash for you. And latterly something else, I believe.'

Simpson smiled thinly. 'We were under the fond delusion that Backlash was top secret. How come you can bandy the name about?'

'It's my trade,' I explained. 'I'm the chap that people like you call in at short notice, so I have to do my homework. What happened to Tiverton?'

'Car smash, Tuesday night. He was driving himself back from the Eastbourne jamboree. There was a paragraph or two in the papers.'

'Must have missed them. Or maybe it's just that I never read the names of the victims in car crash news items. Left you in a spot, has it?'

'A black spot,' Simpson confirmed briefly.

I took up a stand with my shoulder-blades to the window, watching him glance through a folder. Suddenly he pushed it aside as though it had lost interest for him.

'The fact is, a highly promising operation has been nipped in the bud.'

'Bothersome,' I remarked. 'But you've other gifted researchers on your strength, I take it. Why call on me? I was never in Tiverton's class.'

'Exactly.'

The reply was cryptic enough to make me wait. Having sent me a swift look to check that I was listening, Simpson picked up a wooden ruler from his desk and slid it noisily along his front teeth while redirecting his gaze at a huge wall-chart which appeared to show the progress of a number of technical programmes. Some of the graph-lines were levelling out.

'You're not known,' he observed, 'as a scientist. In fact you're barely known at all. You've kept it that way. You're about as faceless as anyone could be. This suits us fine.'

'I'm glad. Mind telling me how it helps?'

He waited a few moments. 'Tiverton worked on Backlash for us, as you said just now. He and his team had a big success. Naturally, the other side knew of this – '

'Other side?'

'I'm sure I don't have to elaborate.'

'As the pulp fiction market has it. All right. The vernacular is accepted.'

'Thank you.' The sarcasm was acidulated as only he could make it. 'Backlash, as you doubtless have made it your business to know, represents a revolution in tank warfare. Most of our potential foes would dearly like to possess something comparable, but we happen to know they're way behind. We'd like them to stay there.'

'Spiteful.'

'It occurred to us,' said Simpson with an extra gallop on the dental scales, 'that a good way of ensuring this might be to send them off on a completely wrong track.'

I sniffed cautiously. 'Can't fault the reasoning. How about the execution?'

'Our plan,' he said coolly, 'was that John Tiverton should defect.'

'I see. And was he about to oblige?'

'It was all fixed up. With his and our connivance, of course. He'd no actual wish to defect: what we'd agreed was that he should pretend to do so, work for them for a year or so, perpetrating a few subtle errors that would wreck their project, then defect back . . .'

'If he could.'

'We'd made all the arrangements. There wasn't much risk.'

'Who's we?'

'The Service and myself.'

'Who are you operating through?'

'A man called Phillison who's been with us for years. He has contact with the other side: they think he's with them.'

'And of course he's nothing of the sort?' I kept most but not all of the irony out of my voice.

'He's been triple-screened,' Simpson said testily.

'That's grand, then.'

'I'll vouch for him personally. I don't do that with many, as you know. Anyway, that was the scheme.' He paused. 'Then Tiverton has to get himself killed.'

'Frightfully disobliging. You've applied for his re-incarnation?'

'I'm doing so,' he said quietly, 'at this moment.'

I stared at him.

'Are you barmy? How could I possibly deputize for someone of Tiverton's calibre?'

'I'm not asking you to deputize. Reincarnation, you

said. I want you to *be* Tiverton: literally step into his shoes, defect, and carry out the programme he was scheduled for.'

For a second or two I was speechless.

'But they know what he looked like! I don't bear any resemblance.'

'You're much the same height and build.'

'But the face!'

He arched the ruler, producing a splitting sound. 'That's where the car crash comes in. Tiverton's face was shattered, you see. Beyond recognition.'

'Also he was killed.'

'That's what the papers said. But we know better, don't we?'

I made a scoffing noise in the back of my throat. 'You imagine they'd fall for that?'

'They have already.' He leaned back complacently. 'Phillison has dropped the word: Tiverton survived the crash and is being patched up; then he'll defect to them as arranged. With a new face.'

'They'll never swallow it.'

'Why not? Provided the man who turns up has Tiverton's personality and background, can answer accurately any question put to him about his former life and can handle their project with apparent authority . . . what's to prevent it?'

I thought for a moment. 'Tiverton's death has been reported, you say. There'll be a funeral and an inquest. What are the other side going to think was used for a body?'

Simpson pressed a desk-buzzer. Pushing back his chair, he dragged out a drawer to produce an oval tin of slim cigars, one of which he extracted and lit. As an afterthought he waved the tin; I signalled back a negative.

Presently the office door opened to admit a middle-aged man of mild demeanour who reclosed it scrupulously behind him before taking up a semi-apologetic stance in front of it and dividing a look of respectful inquiry between us. I stayed at the window, out of the beam of Simpson's desk-lamp.

'This,' said Simpson, 'is Tony Phillison. Tell my visitor, Tony, how we explain about the body.'

With a precise delivery, Phillison recounted the story which, according to his chief, he had already transmitted to the 'other side'. Tiverton, the tale ran, had picked up a hitch-hiker on his way from Eastbourne on the Tuesday night, and it was this man who had died in the crash. Tiverton himself had regained consciousness in time to slip his wallet and other belongings into the dead man's pockets; subsequently this had led to false identification, assisted by the fact that the hitch-hiker's face had been smashed as well.

Tiverton had then staggered away to seek help privately from a medical friend who lived in a nearby village. The medical friend, told that Tiverton wanted to vanish for domestic reasons, had agreed to make secret arrangements for plastic surgery over a period of months.

'Ingenious,' I pronounced. 'And totally implausible.'

Simpson said, 'Why?'

'I'd never believe it. Why should they?'

'They don't have to – not all at once. They can wait and accept a defector calling himself John Tiverton the metallurgist: once they've got him, they can put him to the test. If he can pass that test . . .'

Simpson brandished the ruler.

Taking the gesture apparently as a dismissal, Phillison withdrew silently, fastening the door with the same feline delicacy of touch as that with which he had arrived.

Once more throwing himself back in his chair, Simpson
stared at me challengingly.

'Well?'

'It's lunatic,' I told him.

'Lunacy has triumphed before. What about some of
the World War Two deceptions? If it was done with
enough conviction, a masquerade like this could be even
more successful in a way than our original plan . . .'

'How?'

'For one thing, there'd be no risk of your changing
your mind and opting to stay with them, as Tiverton
might conceivably have done. You never know.'

'My changing *my* mind?'

'We want you to do it,' he said, as though asking me
to organize a tennis tournament. 'What we're offering is a
very good proposition indeed, and I'd like you to consider
it.'

The offer was every bit as good as Simpson had indicated.
For form's sake I haggled a little, although in fact I had
decided on the spot to take it up.

The danger element seemed acceptable. Even if the
scepticism of my bona fides proved too acute to be over-
ridden, I could always explain with a shrug to the 'other
side' that I had wanted to defect anyway, and had
reasoned that I stood a better chance by posing as a more
illustrious figure. As Charles Thomas, I had enough
scientific qualifications to be of some use to them . . .
until I could find a means of getting out.

And if escape proved impossible, that wouldn't bother
me too much. I had no ties in the West. No family, no
close friends; no politics, no axes to grind. I was a loner.
The exchange of one form of free-lancing for another
would be no special hardship. And while it would be a

pity to forgo the plump sum I had been promised on completion of the mission, I felt sure that, in these slightly more enlightened times, opportunities of an equivalently profitable nature must exist behind the Iron Curtain.

Taking my decision in his faintly arrogant fashion as a matter of course, Simpson proceeded to the briefing.

I had, he explained, several months in which to soak myself in Tiverton's existence. There had to be a delay, to enable the mythical facial surgery to be carried out and the 'scars' to heal. I could use the time by absorbing everything there was to be learned about Tiverton's work, career, domestic state, life-style, character, fads and fancies.

Material was not lacking.

Tiverton, it seemed, had been the confiding type, and one of his chief confidants had been Simpson himself, whom he appeared to have regarded as a kind of father-confessor and marriage counsellor as well as overlord.

There was also an inch-thick dossier on him, prepared by the security boys when he was being screened for Backlash. Other information had come from people like Frank Selby, Phillison – and Sally Masters, but indirectly, via Joan Petworth, whom she had kept fully informed of her man-devouring exploits. Joan had a direct line to Simpson, who found her invaluable as a source of latently explosive information concerning his staff, and encouraged her prying.

All this amounted to sufficient to keep us – Simpson and me – fully stretched at a series of briefing sessions during which he did his utmost to open Tiverton's soul for my inspection.

There were even tapes of the man's voice, recorded as routine in the course of interviews in Simpson's office. I was told to listen and relisten to them, assimilate the

timbre and inflection, pick up the dialect, adopt Tiverton's
verbal mannerisms and his approach to a dialogue.
Photographs of his wife, Valerie, and their two children
were likewise available.

The more intimate domestic details, of course, were the
hardest of all to amplify. Outline facts were known,
since Tiverton had described many of them – including
the wedding day farce – either to Sally Masters or to
Simpson himself, and had not been backward in analysing
his own emotions and reactions at various times.

With regard to Valerie's, he had not unnaturally been
less explicit. Simpson surmounted this difficulty in some
degree by calling upon her after a decent interval to offer
his personal condolences on her husband's death; he
had a way with him which exerted its spell. After some
initial reticence, Valerie laid bare her heart.

Simpson conscientiously relayed everything in my
direction.

The ingestion of daunting amounts of variegated data
was second nature to me. The facility had been my
stock-in-trade since the time I had walked out of my first
and only regular employment, as scientific marketing
adviser to a toy manufacturer in Leeds. With my parents
dead and no other immediate family, I had found that it
suited my nature to live anonymously, accepting com-
missions of almost any nature that came along, legal or
otherwise (I drew a fixed line of my own between technical
transgressions and criminality). There was no shortage of
work.

In the early days, an especially rewarding field was that
of cosmetics. A few of the pirate dabblers in this diamond-
mine of an industry found it helpful to be able to call
upon somebody discreet who could knock them up a
quick, cheap concoction that could be marketed in glossy

wrappers as the latest ultimate in anti-perspirants or under-arm deodorants, relatively non-toxic if inherently impotent; and I made sure I was readily at hand to oblige. From this I had progressed to other covert assignments embracing a range of functions, acquiring a reputation for reliability – I was, after all, a B.Sc. and had a retentive mind – plus absolute discretion. As far as it went, I offered value. For hard cash.

Thus I was no stranger to mugging up a subject for a specific purpose. But stepping into the skin of another man was a different piece of fruit cake.

Everyone should try it some time. The number of separate items of knowledge that can be gleaned about any single human being would be frightening if it were assessable. The security dossier alone took me a week to commit to memory: on top of this, Simpson was feeding me supplementary facts in a ceaseless cascade, testing me on them whenever we met, and always adding to the store. Within a month, I found that I was beginning to think no longer as Charles Thomas. I regarded myself as John Tiverton.

The metamorphosis was deliberate. It simplified the undertaking. My identity as Thomas was far from notable: I had achieved nothing of which I was proud enough to want to lock away in my personality. Tiverton, on the other hand, was an interesting study. He had done a lot; he had a wife and family; possessing none of my own, I conceived a proprietary attitude towards this woman and these children whom I had never met, and began concurrently to involve myself in the history of his private relationships and his career with Kaltmans.

Subconsciously, I think, I harboured the notion of stepping actually into his shoes when the job itself was done. It was no sacrifice to let slip the image of Thomas and replace it with this new, more intriguing, altogether more complete example of humanity. The situation he had occupied until his death became more real, more immediate to me than my own had ever been. And so it became progressively easier to learn.

In parallel with this, it was necessary that I should be familiarized thoroughly with Backlash. This itself was merely the preliminary to mastering the numerous subtle divergencies from the true process that I was going to have to build into the project, if and when I was put in charge of it by the 'other side'. It had to seem authentic, and yet the alterations had to be so fundamental as to sabotage the operation. Such scientific training as I had had was light-years from this; I was forced to start from scratch and learn parrot-fashion.

By the third month I was word-perfect. I was even offering suggestions of my own for additional eye-washing of the opposition, as I knew Tiverton would have done. I knew all about him. I knew what his response would have been to any given stimulus. I was behaving as he would have behaved: my mental and bodily functioning was his. I was Tiverton.

No trouble was spared. Following a remark of mine that it might have been helpful to have some knowledge of the interior of the Tivertons' house, Simpson one morning smugly handed me some prints. Apparently, as part of the screening process on Tiverton, someone had been sent along to pose as a rates inspector and obtain some filmed shots of the rooms. The exact reason for this was obscure: it had something to do with ascertaining Tiverton's tastes in home reading. The man who went was clumsy about it, but he did manage to put on celluloid the hall and kitchen as well as the living-room from outside the french door, before Valerie's mounting suspi-

cion frightened him off. By studying the pictures I formed
a reasonable impression of the layout. It looked like a
pleasant house. The kind I should not have minded
owning myself, if I had had someone to share it with.

Phillison I met only once more: briefly, as I sat in the
back of a taxi in Albemarle Street off Piccadilly where he
handed me some literature that Simpson wanted me to
see urgently. Apart from this he kept out of sight. I
understood that he was maintaining contact with 'the
other crowd', keeping them on the boil, assuring them of
the eventual delivery of Tiverton, complete with a new
face and an established stockpile of priceless expertise.

In the first week of the fourth month, the unforeseen
occurred.

CHAPTER 20

Mrs Carpenter stirred.

'What happened?'

'Before I tell you,' I said, 'I want to explain about
the notebook.'

'I don't think you have to. They're notes you made to
help you remember the various details?'

I nodded. 'In the early stages it seemed like a sound
idea – but I soon gave up. There was just too much to
put on paper. That half-filled notebook represents
approximately one hour's briefing. It's mainly trivia.
For example, this bit . . .'

Opening the notebook at the page containing the entry
that had first caught my eye, I passed it to her. She read
out the gibberish: 'Sp ls – kprs, bl cf, sw t. Rl-nk swrs.
H bs. Sp dsl – b eggs.'

With raised eyebrows she glanced up.

I translated: 'Special likes – kippers, black coffee, sweet tea. Roll-neck sweaters. Hot baths. Special dislike – boiled eggs.'

'Pretty banal,' she said with a laugh.

'That's Tiverton himself. Over the page – ' I turned a leaf – 'are some ciphers relating to the children. Barbara – one six three six nine . . . that's her date of birth, sixteenth of March nineteen sixty-nine. And then it goes on to describe her a bit – flaxen hair, slim, blue eyes. And Michael; brown hair, chubby, green eyes, slight limp.' I handed her the book again. 'After that we really got down to detail. It would have needed a hundred books that size to contain it all.'

After a brief inspection of other pages she laid the notebook on the trolley. 'Yes, I see. So you decided to rely on memory?'

'In the end,' I said drily, 'you have to. But as it turned out, it was just this that let me down. After the accident.'

She waited in silence.

'I told you how I was in the library reading-room, looking up something on metal alloys. This was the evening before last. By that time, as I said, I was consciously thinking of myself as Tiverton – I remember I even went up to one of his professional acquaintances, a fellow called Brent, expecting him to recognize me; of course he didn't know me from Adam. This shows you my mental and psychological condition at that stage.'

She nodded, her eyes fixed upon me. 'The mind can make these enormous jumps. I've seen it.'

'You know the phrase "entering into the spirit of the thing" – I'd entered into the spirit of Tiverton, quite literally. There's no question of that. Well, finally it got too stuffy for me in there, and so I left with the book and went downstairs and out into the street . . . and that's when it happened.'

'What did?'

'I was standing on the edge of the pavement, trying to remember if there was something I'd meant to buy on the way home. My home, that is – the flat I occupied as Charles Thomas in Bayswater. Suddenly I found myself lying on the footpath. Some woman was bending over me, asking me if I was all right. I told her I was – I did feel a bit shaken up, but otherwise fine.'

'A black-out,' speculated Mrs Carpenter.

'That was my first thought. But it turned out that I'd got in the way of a car trying to do a fast U-turn: the driver misjudged his clearance and the offside wing nicked me as it came round, sent me head-first into a plate-glass window.'

'The stupid man!'

'He was most contrite about it. Anyway I was helped up, dusted down, asked if I felt fit to travel home . . . I think I may have brushed them off a bit touchily, though I can't be sure. This is the part that's still a bit hazy.'

'The shock – '

'It wasn't that exactly. I felt quite okay in myself, perfectly well, not even a headache; I just wanted them to leave me alone so that I could get home. I wanted Valerie to know I was all right.'

Mrs Carpenter stared. I smiled at her.

'You see what had occurred? That bump on the head from the plate-glass window had completed the process: it scattered the vestiges of Charles Thomas and left me with the identity uppermost in my consciousness – Tiverton's. It was his house I travelled back to, fully expecting a cosy welcome from Valerie and the kids.

What I got, of course . . .'

'Utter blankness. How terrible for you.'

'So that's how it all started. The more I tried to rationalize anything, the more bewildering it became. No wonder Valerie was scared. Poor girl, she'd never seen me before in her life. She knew her real husband was dead. What she didn't know was the first thing about Simpson's revised plan. And apart from Phillison and, I suppose, a handful of others in some cagey department, nobody else did either.'

'Of all the impossible positions,' Mrs Carpenter said in a low voice.

We were silent for a while. At last I got to my feet, set off on a restless prowl of the room, scanning the book titles on the shelves without recording them.

'Looking back now, with the block cleared, I wonder how I could have failed to realize. But of course it's not that simple.'

'Of course not.'

'It's as you said: weird things can take place in the mind. Short of a drastic antidote – like my nosedive into a wall just now – there's often no way back.'

She remained seated, watching me. 'What are you going to do?'

I halted, staring down at the stereo turntable. It nursed a recording of arias from *Tosca* sung by Louise Fisher, the young English soprano discovered at a contest held four years previously in Huddersfield. I wondered what she sounded like from two loudspeakers in a smallish room. It was no test of a voice.

'I'm not sure,' I mumbled.

Mrs Carpenter stood. 'Can I offer some advice?'

'I wish you would.'

'Go upstairs and get a night's sleep. In the morning,

after breakfast, travel over to Kaltmans, present yourself again to Melville Simpson – '

'No.' My head shook. 'I don't think I shall do that.'

'Why ever not?' Amazement suffused her face. 'You've got it straightened out now: you can explain – '

'I want time first. Time to weigh up my future.'

I pivoted to look at her. 'I've blown the entire thing, you see. Hiked around prematurely to everyone, claiming to be Tiverton. Simpson's not going to like that. Neither are the security mob. They could get vindictive.'

'Surely not.'

I laughed harshly. 'You don't know this trade. Nor do I, to that extent . . . but I'm learning. I've got to be alone for a few days or weeks, so that I can decide on the best course.'

She studied me doubtfully. 'If you're convinced that's the wisest policy. I should certainly sleep on it first; you may feel differently tomorrow. You've been through a lot. If you do decide to lie low for a while . . . where will you make for?'

Concern shadowed her eyes. She looked compact and staunch, standing there in sweater and trousers; a good sort to have around. I said, 'Will the attic bedroom still be available after tonight?'

CHAPTER 21

The grinding moan of small-hours traffic reached me from the streets, four floors below.

A lorry; a car or two; a second lorry. I lay counting them, registering them on a mental chart.

Stillness gathered up its skirts and held its breath.

My eyes were caught by something. The faintest flutter of the curtain. I tried vainly to ignore it. The movement was an intrusion, an irritant: there was a stealthiness about it that was worse than a noisy flapping. Presently I threw back the bedclothes. Hauling myself over the yielding springs to the window, I pulled it shut with a clump, jammed the stay into place.

Outside, the lighted ocean gleamed at me.

Crawling back, I tucked myself in.

Notwithstanding the closure of the window, the room seemed still not entirely soundless. Raising my head from the pillow (it was the foam rubber kind, springy and uncomfortable) I peered at the closet doors: in the half-light it was difficult to be certain. Although I had tied them again with a sock, one or both of them could have come off the catch. Freeing myself once more from the sheets, I padded across the carpet.

The doors were tight in the frame. There was nothing more inside the room to create a stir.

Unless it was the plumbing.

After some hesitation I went over to the washbasin and tried the taps. Both were turned fully off. I had ensured this before going to bed: dripping taps are an abomination.

Perhaps it was in the pipes.

I put the question to myself: what was it I could hear? The answer had to be – nothing. There was no audible disturbance that I could have pinpointed. It was more of a sensation: the kind that might communicate itself to a maggot if someone began very gently squeezing the apple.

As I moved away from the taps, my ears picked up a creak.

Attic rooms in elderly buildings were notorious for

loose boards under carpets. I threw weight on to one foot, searching for the culprit, unable to reproduce the sound. With mounting urgency I tried again, repeatedly, pressing upon sundry spots with the ball of a foot: it was vital that I should hear that creak a second time. I couldn't make it happen.

When I gave up experimenting I was facing the door. Intent upon the floorboards, I had given it no attention; now, as my eyes focused, it seemed to me that it was moving very slightly in its frame. Or – revising my immediate impression – giving the faintest of shudders. Barely had the idea formed before its cause evaporated; the door shed its minimal vibrancy, became rock-still, like a predator freezing.

A draught from the staircase would have done it.

The proposition was a comforting one. Except that no draught would exist unless the fire-door on the lower landing had been opened against its spring; in which case, upon release it would close itself again. Unless it were held.

Reaching out for the wall-switch, I snapped on the light.

The click seemed to awaken echoes. It was as though half a dozen mice, roused by the rasp of metal, had decided upon a small furtive excursion to investigate. But almost before the activity had come into existence, it was snuffed out. Listen as I might, I could detect no further movement; I was less than certain that I had heard any. I came away from the switch. The legs of the pyjamas I was wearing brushed together, causing me to wonder whether all the half-sounds and quarter-flutters were attributable to this single origin; whether my imagination had become inflamed to a point where a heartbeat could be equated with tramping boots. Untying the cord,

I stepped out of the pyjamas and, returning to the bed, gathered my clothes together. I started to dress.

The zip of the trousers caught halfway. Struggling to free it, I heard a soft thump from outside the door. This time there could be no question. It was followed by tiny scuffing movements and, to my pricked ears, a muffled word or two. I moved back to the centre of the room.

'Who's there?' I called sharply.

There was a sound like an exclamation, involuntary and suppressed. With a savage tug I got the zip to waist-level, stepped into my shoes. I had my jacket in my hands, hunting for the first armhole, when the door shuddered to an impact. The bolt was a small one: its screws came half out of their sockets in a noise of splitting woodwork. My instinct was to jump back. Overcoming it, I advanced to lend my weight to the defences, but before I could reach the door-handle there was a second concussion, the bolt flew out of its seating and the door burst inwards, striking my arm to send me reeling backwards into a sprawling position on the bed.

Two of them came into the room. The first, staggering from his own momentum, fetched up against the wash-basin where he hung on for a moment while the second rushed at me. By a contortion of the body I avoided being pinned to the mattress: his weight landed on my left arm, but I dragged it clear and got to my feet. The other stood between me and the door. His grasp was strong. But the vigour of desperation had invaded my own sinew; with a wild delight I sent him reeling again, wrenched my lapel from his fingers and made a dive for the staircase. Midway down, blocking the way to the fire-door, stood a third.

Swinging myself from the handrails I flung out both feet, kicking him in the face before my ankles were grabbed and held. I threshed violently.

As his grip weakened, my arms were pinioned from above. This time no sort of struggle could release them although I twisted like a circus performer, feeling the dead hopelessness of impotent effort, the horror of total restriction. Only one course remained open. I filled my lungs.

'Help!' I screamed. 'Please help me, somebody!'

Behind me a voice swore. 'He can pack that in, for Christ's sake. Wake the bloody neighbourhood.'

'Shut *up*, Tiverton.' A second voice. 'It'll do you no good. You're coming with us.'

'Thomas.' I saw no reason to perpetuate the subterfuge. 'I'm Charles Thomas.' The words were shaken out of me as I was hoisted into a semi-horizontal position and carried down past the open fire-door to the third-floor landing. Heads peered from bedroom doors. As we went by I appealed to them. 'I'm being kidnapped! Stop them, can't you?'

It was like speaking through plate-glass to shop dummies. The looks of petrified blankness on their idiot faces filled me with a fury that was chilled by the sluggish tributary of fear. 'For God's sake . . .' My voice was a futile squeak. 'Can't one of you *do* something? Don't you see what's happening?'

Stolidly my captors went on carrying me down like a sack of potatoes. Nobody got in their way. Abruptly it dawned upon me why: the one ahead of me, holding my ankles, wore the disguise of a policeman, perfect to the last detail. They were smart; their resource was unlimited. From the floors above came a rising murmur of speculative voices: they were actually discussing the incident as it took place. I struggled some more, but my strength was draining away like water through muslin. As we reached the ground-floor passage I became still, counting upon their need to set me down for a breather; this would give Mrs Carpenter some opportunity to organize something.

Wrapped in a cherry-red house-robe, she was standing next to the table with its visiting cards and its Guides to London. The look she turned upon me was strange. It comprised outrage and curiosity plus an element of smug relish, the sight of which turned my blood to ice. Aware that for some reason it was useless, I made my expression one of entreaty. 'Can't you please get help? You know the situation I'm in.'

A man in a bulky greatcoat eased himself past her. His fur-lined collar was up around his neck and the tip of his nose was pink. 'What situation would that be, Tiverton?'

'Thomas,' I insisted. 'Charles Thomas. Ask her – she knows.'

He turned to her. 'You say he arrived last night?'

'That's right.' Her tone was forthright, unemotional. 'Quite late, with no luggage.'

'And you remembered him?'

'Yes, from a year or so back.'

'He'd stayed here previously?'

'For a few days.' She flung me a glance. 'This time he looked so odd, I thought, Hullo, what's he been up to? He gave me a false name. I knew that, because I looked up the name he'd registered under before. John Tiverton.'

'And then you watched the late news on TV?'

'Right. And the penny dropped.'

With a nod he turned back. There was a disturbing hint of compassion in the way he looked down at me. 'John Tiverton,' he said quietly, 'you're under arrest.'

'Arrest?' I cried. 'You have to be joking. What for, in heaven's name?'

'For the murder of your wife, Valerie, and of your neighbour, Thomas Elkins.'

CHAPTER 22

Their cleverness is nothing short of diabolical.

Somehow, by God knows what manipulation of cash or influence, they have contrived almost overnight to set up this remarkable establishment in which to have me kept under lock and key, isolated from reality, while they chisel with delicate artistry at the mass of my narrative, striving to persuade me that parts need reshaping.

The entire thing is being tackled with supreme skill. In the course of the next few pages I shall hope to show the ingenuity with which they have taken the lifestyle of the noted physicist, John Tiverton, in the year preceding his death, and turned it to account in endeavouring to merge our separate identities, his and mine.

Perhaps a prime example of their technique can be found in the conversations I have had with an individual who has visited me on several occasions during the past few weeks. Tiler, he calls himself. He claims to be my 'defence solicitor'. He has requested that I am fully frank with him: so I am fully frank, to the point of obsessiveness, and he believes not a syllable of what I say . . . or so he pretends. He puts 'searching' questions.

'But it's true, isn't it, Mr Tiverton, that you had a lasting relationship with Sally Masters which your wife came to know about?'

'Thomas,' I remind him. 'My name is Charles Thomas.

As far as I know, Tiverton did have an affair with her . . . though it's only what I've been told.'

'But by your own admission – '

'I know. When I called on her that afternoon she took me into her bed. I've explained why.'

'At the flat in Highgate, you mean? Where you say she lives with her husband, Douglas Clark?'

'Right.'

'But she isn't married.' His walrus moustache droops at me. 'She lives there alone.'

I say contemptuously, 'This is what Simpson tells you?'

'It's a fact,' he murmurs.

Caressing the moustache, he reflects: pounces again. 'You'd been under intense strain, hadn't you, on the Backlash project?'

'Tiverton had.'

'Months of severe mental application, pressure from superiors, the tension that arose from heading a talented but temperamental research team. And on top of it all, a domestic situation which . . . It had all become too much, isn't that right?'

I shrug. 'Tiverton could have told you. If he hadn't died.'

'There was no crash in Sussex,' he intones. 'No inquest. No report in any newspaper.'

I say nothing. There seems little point.

He assumes a confidential air. 'Tell me this. If you're *not* Tiverton, why do you say that when the child Barbara woke up in bed and saw you, she blurted out "Hallo, Daddy"?'

'She'd only recently lost her father,' I point out. 'Wouldn't it be natural for any child, coming out of a sleep and finding a man bending over her, to assume it was her daddy come back?'

There is a very long pause.

'You must be open with me, Mr Tiverton. I can prepare some sort of a defence so long as I have all the facts.'

'I've given them to you.'

He sighs. Lengthily but soundlessly. Shakes his head.

I sit looking at him, coldly admiring his act. I suppose him to be yet another of Simpson's lackeys. How many has the man got?

Simpson himself has had the gall to visit me. When I first saw him waiting there in that bald room, my spirits soared; I thought he had come to engineer my release. But it speedily became clear what he was up to.

I interrupted his opening remarks to say, 'You may as well forget the "John" nonsense. There's no point to it any more.'

My directness seemed to disconcert him. 'I've told them everything I can,' he said presently, examining me as though I were something under glass. 'They're prepared to give you an easy ride, I'm positive, so long as – '

'Told them everything? What does that mean?'

'The stress you were under. That year on Backlash. I've done all I can to make clear that what you did was totally out of character, brought on by – '

'Now look, Simpson.' He did look, with a humility that didn't fool me for an instant but merely stoked my burning inner rage. 'I don't know what you still hope to salvage from this operation, but I can tell you I don't appreciate being one of the waste pieces thrown into the scrap bin. If and when I'm brought to trial in a bona fide court of law on this trumped-up charge, I warn you I shall blow the lot: and to hell with the Official Secrets Act. So before you start considering me expendable, chew on that.'

He made a show of looking unhappy, at a loss.

'John, I don't get it. How would spilling details of Backlash help you in – '

'As we both well know,' I said significantly, 'it's not Backlash itself that we're talking about. And will you stop calling me John? You know damn well who I am.'

This time it was the frankly bemused expression. He does it so well.

'I can't see your purpose,' he complained, 'in keeping up this extraordinary fiction. I knew Charles Thomas as well as you did . . . which wasn't all that well. We've had no contact with him for eighteen months or more. The word is he's gone abroad.'

'I'm aware,' I said bitingly, 'what the word is. Handily put about, wasn't it? To tie in with the mission.'

'*Mission?*' His mouth hung agape. 'What in hell are you on about?'

At this point, I think, I may have begun to shout. Mostly I have kept control, but there are limits beyond which I find it hard to be pushed. My last, blurred impression of Simpson is of seeing him, steadfastly performing his pale and shaken act, being sponsored from the room by an amazingly large 'policeman' in full dress. I have not set eyes on him since.

No doubt he is keeping a low profile, still nursing hopes of safeguarding his precious cover with a view to launching some heavily-revised operation in the immediate future. He may have a disagreeable surprise or two in store.

Apart from Tiler, who calls weekly, the person I have seen the most of is a rather bland character of about fifty, with silver-shot hair swept back over his ears, and a pair of pale blue eyes that suffer permanently from an unexcited proptosis as we converse. He has never introduced himself. He appears to assume that I shall feel motivated to confide in him, anonymous as he remains.

While bearing in mind the perils, I find it a relief to talk to someone. At least, unlike Tiler, he seems to find it unnecessary to contradict my remarks. On the contrary, he expresses great interest in them.

At our most recent meeting I told him: 'The witness who could really help, if I could see her for just a few minutes, is Tiverton's wife, Valerie.'

He regarded me for a few seconds. 'Where do you believe her to be?'

'I keep telling everyone: she's taken the children off somewhere. Surely it's not impossible to have her traced?'

He made a note on a pad. 'And Thomas Elkins?'

'If he hasn't come forward voluntarily,' I said, 'he must have reasons of his own. He's done nothing culpable as far as I'm aware.'

'You feel no animosity towards him?'

'Why should I?'

'Would you accept, though, that the man called John Tiverton might have had reason to?'

'That I couldn't possibly say. I only know what I've been told about him.'

He made another note. 'By the way,' he added, glancing up, 'I'd be interested to see this notebook you've spoken of: the one containing the cryptic entries. Any idea who has it at the moment?'

I managed a bitter smile. 'I'm informed it doesn't exist. In other words, it's conveniently vanished. No doubt Simpson saw to that.'

'You think so?'

'He must have got at the Carpenter woman. She was the last to handle it.'

'What are your feelings,' he asked, 'towards Mrs Carpenter?'

'Unquotable.'

'You feel she . . . let you down?'

'That's hardly the expression. She betrayed me.'

He mused. 'During the night you spent at her hotel – '

'I was there two nights.'

'One, according to her.'

'She's lying, of course.'

More notes. The pale eyes protruded at me again.

'A great many people about you seem to be telling untruths.'

'There's a great deal at stake,' I said meaningfully. 'More even than I'd grasped, possibly. The vastness of this conspiracy is only just starting to dawn on me.' I thumped the table. 'This is why I've got to have the chance to present the true facts – make them known publicly, before the most incredible injustice is done. You can see that, can't you?'

The inclination of his head was non-committal. It convinced me, if nothing else had, that there was nothing he would or could do; like the rest, he was a puppet. A kind of weary obstinacy made me add: 'To do this I must get bail – so that I can search for people like Valerie Tiverton and Elkins, make contact with them, persuade them to speak up. You see the urgency?'

Pocketing the notepad, he stood.

'I'll be back to see you again.' It was the platitude of a surgeon to a terminally-ill patient. There was an aura of resignation about him as he left the room.

A day or two later came the confrontation that I want to describe more fully. It has a particular significance, I believe, not only in its content but also in its style. The markings it bears are those of a subtle flank attack, meticulously schemed, calculated to sow confusion.

From the beginning this was evident. Of the two who

faced me in that same spartan room, the spokesman – he
posed as a chief-superintendent – adopted at first a friendly
manner, offering cigarettes, asking me to make myself
comfortable, couching his opening questions in the gentlest
of undertones as though he wished neither them nor my
replies to reach the ears of his companion, seated more
distantly with a large notebook on his knee. It was done
with sinister expertise.

'I appreciate,' he began, 'that you've been asked this
before: but for the record I'd like you to tell me personally,
man to man. What is your *full* name?'

I was nearly disarmed. I tried to keep any answering
friendliness out of my voice. 'Charles Thomas.'

'Thank you,' he said courteously. 'Now I want to
ask you something about events which occurred towards
the end of last month. I shall be quite specific and I'd
like you to reply in kind. Fair enough?'

Instead of reassurance I was finding nothing but
menace in his approach. I tried not to show it. For the
moment it seemed advisable to humour them, to give an
impression of being duped by the procedure. 'Go ahead,'
I invited.

He paused, as though marshalling his brief. I could
well believe that he had to. There was a lot for him to
remember.

'On a day,' he commenced eventually, 'in the latter
part of October – the twenty-second – you were in the
reading-room of the Barton Street Library off Tottenham
Court Road, engaged in some research?'

'Correct.'

'At about four forty-five you left the building, taking
with you the volume you had been studying – Kummel's
Theses.' He waited briefly for a possible denial. 'What
happened after that?'

I considered. 'I was involved in a slight accident.'

'What form did that take?'

'A car brushed me. I've related this several times. I fell across the footpath and hit my head on a shop window.'

Deadpan, he said, 'And then?'

'I went home.'

'What did you find there?'

'I found my wife. Or so I believed at the time.'

'You mean it wasn't her?'

The other man glanced across at us. His pen was travelling smoothly.

I said, 'Of course it wasn't.'

'Who was it, then?'

'Do I have to go through the farce of telling you? It was Valerie Tiverton. John Tiverton's wife.'

The 'superintendent' took a quiet pull at his cigarette. 'You maintain that you don't know this Mr Tiverton?'

'I never knew him personally.'

'Nor his wife?'

'No: and she didn't know me.'

Although his cigarette was only half-smoked, he crushed its ignited tip into a veined china ashtray to his left, taking his time about it as though summoning concentration. When he spoke again his voice had undergone a noticeable alteration; it was level, and there was steel in its constitution.

'Climb off it, Tiverton. Isn't it time you gave up?'

'Gave up what?' I sensed that we had reached a new phase. I was ready for him.

'This pretence,' he said with a show of anger. 'In the view of the psychiatrist you're not confused: just clever.'

'That's flattering.'

'You think you can pull the wool over everyone's eyes ... but mine, you'll find, are in the back of my head.

Now what about it? Are you going to tell us what happened?'

'I've told your accomplices. Several times, in detail.'

'What you've told us is an elaborate fantasy.' He waited.
'All right.' He leaned forward. 'I'm going to tell *you*
what happened – in detail. Only my details happen to be
the accurate ones.'

Again he waited, possibly hoping for an interjection.
I didn't oblige. Leaving the half-cigarette in the ashtray,
he brought out his packet and selected another, tapping
it carefully on the wrapping.

'You left the library, as you've said; but you weren't
knocked down. That's an invention. You went home and
you found your wife: also you found your neighbour,
Thomas Elkins. The two of them were together in the
front room, with the curtains drawn. You surprised them
making love.'

I met his gaze calmly. 'Seems to be a knack of mine;
surprising people.'

'You'd had a fraught year. At Kaltmans you were
under load on confidential projects. At home, your wife
had recently found out about the liaison between yourself
and your assistant, Sally Masters: there'd been rows.
For the sake of the family you had ended the relationship . . . and then you had begun to suspect that your
wife in her turn had taken a lover, either as consolation
or in revenge. Isn't this why you left the library early
that afternoon? To find out?'

'Keep going,' I told him. 'I'm getting quite intrigued.'

'They weren't expecting you home until your usual
hour, around seven. Elkins's wife was away on a catering
course; your children had been put to bed; the coast was
clear, they thought. But they were wrong, were they not?'

'If you say so.'

'How did they react to discovery? Shame, humiliation? I fancy not. I may be wrong, but I have the idea they did more than brazen it out – they made a joke of it, made fun of you and your prowess as a husband.'

I frowned. 'Never admit,' I told him, 'to the possibility that you could be wrong. It tends to weaken your case.'

Ignoring this, he chuntered on doggedly. 'A man can take practically anything except that. Does it explain why you lost control? I think it does. I think it explains, Mr Tiverton, why you grabbed up that carpet-sweeper which must have been conveniently to hand and used it in a murderous attack on Mr Elkins, dealing him a succession of blows which shattered his skull.'

The pretence of scribbling had been abandoned by his accomplice, who with pen loosely poised was gazing at me with a faraway look as though having bets with himself on the likely strength of my reaction. The impassivity I maintained was, I hope, a disappointment to them both.

'And Mrs Tiverton?' I inquired mildly.

'Your wife tried to escape. In the hall you caught up with her, striking her several times with the sweeper – there were blood-splashes on the wall and carpet – and then pursuing her into the front garden where you completed the attack. Her dying screams brought other neighbours running. They saw you making off along the street.'

He spoke with a complacent assurance which told me that, if need be, he would be able to produce a neighbour or two who had been prudently bought. I performed a soft clapping of the hands. Applaudingly I said, 'Someone among your crowd has got imagination.'

He shook his head. 'No, Mr Tiverton. You're the one with that.'

Scraping his chair back from the table between us,

he crossed one leg over the other and hugged his chest with both arms, studying my face with a kind of brooding curiosity.

Myself, I didn't stir. 'Not that it seems to weigh,' I remarked, 'so far as you or anyone else here is concerned, but I happen to be Charles Thomas, not this man Tiverton you've been talking about.'

'Your chief at Kaltmans,' he said, apparently switching himself on again, 'has been telling us about you.'

'Me? Or the other chap?'

'He says that aside from your capability as a research scientist, you have an exceptionally vivid imaginative streak . . .'

I laughed shortly. 'From him, of all people.'

'A talent for weaving stories. So what I'm now putting to you, Mr Tiverton — and you've everything to lose and nothing to gain by a denial — is that on this traumatic occasion, in the panic of the moment, you decided to use that talent in a bizarre fashion: to create a fantasy that would interlock with the facts in such a way as to convince everybody that you were not responsible for your actions. And more: that you believed yourself to be someone else entirely.'

His training in psychology showed itself at this moment. The cigarette he had removed from the packet had since lain dormant; now he turned his attention to lighting it, scratching repeatedly at a match, applying the ultimate flame with an expression of absorbed intensity, giving me time to think twice about an instant rebuttal, time to be feebly influenced by the conviction he conveyed. The performance was compelling. I thought it best to keep my silence, to leave the ball in his court; perhaps it would bounce awkwardly, knocking him off balance.

Smoke curved from the cigarette. 'By the end of

that evening there was no lack of factual matter to draw upon. You were, indeed, chased through London. From the public-house where you were first spotted by an off-duty policeman, to a West End cinema and from there to Knightsbridge. Each time you managed to slip the pursuit — although hardly as dramatically as you've described. Certainly you managed to lose yourself in the Albert Hall audience — '

'A one-man show in the gallery,' I couldn't resist putting in.

'I doubt if you did more than enter at the front and leave by the rear. But the story needed a spot of embellishment, didn't it, for your purpose? There was time, plenty of time to think about that after you'd booked in — as Charles Thomas — at Mrs Carpenter's hotel near Victoria.'

I said bitterly, 'You corrupt everyone.'

His eyebrows shot up. 'What do you mean?'

'She was on my side till you got at her. That second evening, I told her the full history and she was going to back me up. What changed her mind? Hard cash, I presume, or else — '

'There was no second evening, Mr Tiverton.'

'Don't insult my intelligence.'

'You were picked up,' he said painstakingly, 'the morning after the killings.'

I gestured. 'Pointless for me to argue.'

'Admittedly, there *had* been an occasion when you did evidently exchange confidences with Mrs Carpenter. That was on your previous visit, more than a year ago: you stayed several days while attending a scientific congress at Caxton Hall. She recalls having a long chat with you over coffee one evening. You had lesser worries at the time. Personal problems. She did her best to advise.'

My slight, weary smile gained no penetration into his armour of sanctimony. He was set on course: nothing was going to halt him.

'What I fail to see,' I told them both impartially, 'is what you basically aim to achieve by all this. Brain-washing? It won't work, you know. I'm not easily deviated.'

'But you think others are.' He threw his henchman a glance. 'Somehow you've fooled yourself that it only needs a sufficiently outlandish restructuring of the under-lying realities to blind us all to the truth. Isn't this it?'

'You're wasting your time.'

'Isn't this the decision you'd reached when you went up to your hotel room that night? That since you'd been witnessed by a number of people in the very act of killing your wife, there was no future in merely denying it: what you needed was a cover story outrageous enough to support an illusion of paranoia. Do you still intend to deny that?'

The inexorability of his build-up induced in me a panicky sensation of nets tightening themselves about my limbs. He was good, this operator. Demonically efficient. I took hold of myself. 'If I were John Tiverton,' I said with what disdain I could muster, 'and I found myself in such a position, why would I pick on Charles Thomas in particular as a fresh identity?'

'Because,' he replied promptly, 'you knew that the real Charles Thomas – who has done free-lance work for Kaltmans in the past – hasn't been seen in this country for close on two years and is thought to have defected to the East.' He squinted towards me. 'Which probably gave you the whole idea.'

'Do let me know,' I requested ironically, 'what other fanciful notions may hit you.'

'Purely deductive reasoning,' he said with daunting

stubbornness. 'The same, only in reverse, as you applied
to creating your story. Everything followed from that
initial device – your arrival home to a blank reception.
Well, that part wasn't so very far from the truth, was it?'

'Are you asking or telling?'

'The rest was made easier by the fact that a good deal
of what you say happened the following day, had actually
occurred earlier.'

'I'm way out of my depth.'

'Although there were subtle differences. Take, for
example, your encounter with Miss Masters in her flat.
I've not the slightest doubt that account was based on a
number of such meetings that did take place when you
and she were on intimate terms. A little judicious doctor-
ing here and there, and presto! – another shiny link in the
fictional chain. In the same way – '

'It may well be,' I interposed hopelessly, 'that Tiverton
went to her flat a good many times. I can only speak for
my own solitary visit, the circumstances of which I've
explained.'

He regarded me in silence. The accomplice jotted a
note.

'The "interviews" with other of your colleagues,' he
resumed at length. 'Weren't they modelled on exchanges
you'd had with them in the past?'

'Suppose I refute it?'

'Mind you,' he went on with a terrible remorseless
perseverance, 'in a few instances you barely needed to
romanticize. You had actually been to Mr Phillison's
house. About six months ago, wasn't it? You looked on
him as an older and wiser head. So you went to him for
advice on your domestic tangle. All you had to do when
this arose was to adapt that conversation . . .'

'Christ,' I murmured long-sufferingly.

'Similarly with your chief, Melville Simpson. He tells us you met once or twice for a drink and a chat in the North Way Lounge of the Hound and Bugle at Hendon: it was while you were at the height of Backlash and he thought it helped you unwind. And on the subject of – '

Angrily I thrust back my chair. I could take no more. 'To hell with you both!' It seemed no longer important that I might be casting whatever advantage I held. 'They may have indoctrinated you, good and solid, but you're not passing it on to me. If someone in the top bracket still hopes to salvage something out of this, you can tell them from me they'll have to go it alone. I'll put up with a lot of things, but a phoney murder rap . . .'

I paused. The two of them were gazing at me with speculative intentness of a type that, I supposed, vindicated their teaching. The immovable proximity of the spokesman repelled me suddenly: rising, I retreated to a corner of the cream-emulsioned room, swung about, stood glaring at them. 'Go away, can't you? Report back to your controllers and leave me alone.'

The 'superintendent' regarded me fixedly from his seat. He continued to speak as though nothing had intervened.

'The home dinner-parties you described. Our inquiries show that they did take place exactly according to your account.'

'What of it?'

'In particular, your version of the second one, the disaster, tallies extremely well with those of Messrs Phillison and Selby. I find it hard to believe that unless you, Mr Tiverton, were actually there yourself on each occasion – '

'What you find hard to believe,' I said through my teeth, 'is of no concern to me. It's immaterial.'

He corrected me quietly. 'On the contrary, it's of the utmost importance to you. Surely you must realize that?'

'I realize I'm shackled hand and foot.'

'It was you that fastened the knots. You know, you're not being too smart. By making an ally of me, you could do yourself a power of good.' The approach had switched again; he was homing in on a new flight-path. 'I'm not in a position to make promises, but it so happens that in my judgement there could well have been a degree of provocation which might – '

'Spare us the crocodile tears.'

My brusqueness threw him. After some delay for recovery he said enticingly, 'Wouldn't you like to know how Barbara and Michael are getting on?'

'Not interested.'

'That I take leave to doubt. Fond of them, aren't you?'

'Fond of two kids I've never seen?'

He gave me a sly look. 'You told us you spoke to Barbara.'

'A couple of words.'

'To which she replied, "Hallo, Daddy."'

'As any child might have.'

'But she's not any child. She's your daughter.'

'Tiverton's daughter.'

He made an obvious effort to govern a rising temper. My immovability was paying off. He started improvising wildly. 'You did once have to climb through Barbara's bedroom window – Miss Cardelaine told us. You'd locked yourself out of the house.'

'Nice try.'

'So that incident got worked into your story, too. But why? It wasn't needed. It tells against you.'

'You explain to me.'

'Right you are. You included the episode as a face-saver. To yourself.'

With lifted shoulders I smiled across at his accomplice. I was running a little low on derisive gestures.

'Subconsciously or otherwise,' he insisted, 'you couldn't tolerate the idea of disowning them entirely. That was the one way you could find of paying lip-service to the truth.'

I laughed aloud.

'And incidentally,' he added, 'of concealing from yourself, maybe, the real sequence of events.'

'Sequence,' I repeated sharply. 'What sequence?'

'The arrival of young Barbara from her room upstairs . . . just in time to see you attacking her mother in the hall.'

With a shake of the head I left my corner to plant both palms on the table, to stare him out. 'They chose well,' I told him.

'Beg pardon?'

'You even *look* like a policeman. And the set-up here . . . it's terrific.'

A frown had lodged between his eyes. 'I'm not with you.'

'All this . . .' I brandished a hand at the walls. 'For my exclusive benefit? Or are there others like me, elsewhere in the place? If not, I'm a bigger fish than I thought.'

For the first time, a trace of uncertainty slipped into his posture. The fund of leading questions had given out. By comparison, his next comeback was the epitome of feebleness.

'What are you giving us now, Tiverton?'

'Thomas,' I amended comfortably, knowing I had won. 'Charles Thomas. I'll give you that; it's all you'll get. The truth? You're not interested. If you were, you'd

have met my demands: found Valerie Tiverton or Tom
Elkins, or both, and brought them here to see me.' With
emphasis I added: 'They'll probably turn up, even now.
The real police are bound to be working on it. And when
they do . . . watch out, that's all. You and your manip-
ulators are going to have some explaining to get through.'

The pair of them exchanged looks.

Momentarily I thought he was about to say something
more: apparently he thought better of it. Coming to his
feet, he stood surveying me for a second or two longer,
perhaps trying to estimate just how far he could go. His
conclusion seemed to be that he had reached the perim-
eter. With a head-jerk to the other, he made for the
door.

I said to their backs, 'If you want to talk sensibly
some other time, you know where I am.'

Since that abortive clash, I have again appeared in
their mock-up of a courtroom to be 'remanded' for the
fourth time. Throughout the sketchy hearing I was
addressed relentlessly by the 'magistrate' as Tiverton.

Apart from my guards, who are elaborately got up in
the uniform of Her Majesty's Prisons (no expense is being
spared in the production of this evil charade), the sole
person I have spoken with during the past few days is
the wretched Tiler, who seems, if anything, more dis-
pirited about things than I am myself. If he really is
supposed to be 'defending' me – against what? – then I
can only say that he has singularly few propositions to
offer. We sit largely in silence.

He has, however, served one vital purpose. At my
request he has brought in a couple of thick writing tablets
on to which, at a furious speed, I have committed this
complete and, I trust, coherent account of recent history

as it concerns myself. Any reasonably attentive study by a person in genuine authority will, I am confident, lead to an investigation and my subsequent release with honour.

My plan to use Tiler to smuggle it out may prove to be a non-starter. Hireling of Simpson though he is, I judge him to be malleable; but I may well be wrong. If this is the case, I shall find some other way. My hopes of Tiler, I confess, are not high. One disheartening factor is that, regardless of all I tell him, he too persists with the utmost conviction in calling me Mr Tiverton. Sometimes I wonder whether he is trying to conceal something from himself. People can be terrifyingly deluded.